RENEGADE

THE FERAL COURT, BOOK II

MYRA DANVERS

FOREWORD

Make sure you sign up for Myra's Newsletter so you never miss sexy NSFW art, free things, exclusive deals, and loads of other cool shit you do not want to miss...

Sign up for Myra's Newsletter today!

This book is dedicated to the eight foot tall portrait of me wearing hexa-breasted armor with a lightning dragon coiled about my feet. In a storm. Standing on a pile of skulls with little bits of brain matter clinging to my boots.
How are they skulls at all if they're still nice and juicy? My dragon is partial to human skin, mmkay?
It's called friggen suspension of disbelief, and it's my money I can do what I want with it!!!
...
On an unrelated note... thanks for buying this book.
You support all of this, so whose fault is it, really?

1

Shifting to ease the ache bunched between her shoulders, she sighed, grumpy at being made to stand and wait. Her fingers twisted in the wisps of fabric swishing about her hips. Bushy tail held stiff at her back, a clear display of irritation she'd stifle the instant she was escorted from the sanctuary of these rooms, for her kind was bred to be submissive. Obedient. Engineered over a thousand generations to suit the biological needs of a species not her own. A much larger, predatory species, yet genetically similar enough to create viable offspring.

The *Anhur*.

Bigger and stronger than her kind, they'd come from the western seas on boats made of bone and found easy prey. Capable of slaughtering the greatest *Hathorian* warrior with a single swipe of deadly claws, the Anhur had indulged themselves. Invading small villages and roaming packs of her ancient kin, they'd taken slaves and obliterated ancient bloodlines at whim.

Entire clans fell in a day. Any females of breeding age were put in chains and sold, the fighting Hathorian males hamstrung. Crippled. Their deadly canines filed short and blunt, while conical, expressive ears were clipped and shaped to suit Anhur fashion.

Left emasculated and utterly unrecognizable as Hathorian without their teeth and ears.

Pillaging resources, the Anhur took as many war brides as they could feed—and gifted the males to their wives as pets to be coddled and displayed. But it didn't take long for those stolen daughters to grow round with the offspring of the conquerors, for the Anhur queens to give birth to unusual kits while their mates were getting rich on the bounty of their conquests.

Hybrids, born bearing the marks of their lineage.

Tiny at birth, they were born in a litter of

their siblings just as pure blooded Hathorian children were.

On their nape, the sparse, dense fur of an Anhur mane traced the top third of the spine.

But as they grew, it became clear these children were different than either species. In adolescences, they stood taller than even their fathers. Their canines grew long and deadly, the only hint that Hathorian blood ran through those massive veins.

It wasn't until the babes matured that the Anhur realized what a gift they truly had.

Hybrids were sterile.

Bigger than their sires with the obedient temperament of their mothers, they were perfect soldiers bred to die in petty wars between Anhur clans. Fighting males incapable of producing offspring of their own *or* threatening pure blooded Anhur children for the rights to inherit their father's holdings. Hybrid females were strong, obedient maidens cherished in the fields and kitchens across the land. Beloved nannies to Anhur children, wet nurses to the many Anhur queens who could afford luxury.

The hybrids transformed Anhur life—and the Hathorians were enslaved by the millions. Stripped of their heritage, their identity... their names. Generations of slaves that would never know anything but *this.*

Sighing, the girl huffed. Impatient to get on with the tedious chore ahead, for though empires had risen and fallen since ancient times, nothing had changed for her people. And she was no different.

Hadim was coming.

The Anhur male who'd claimed the rights to her womb before she'd even been old enough to carry. Her bloodlines were ancient, cultivated over two-thousand years of selective breeding intended to compliment the Karahmet royal family.

Promised before her birth to breed for the most promising son of the Sultan, her children would be sterile hybrids. Betas. Meant to fill the barracks, fight, bleed, and die with honor, but ask nothing for themselves.

It was a dreary life, certainly, but to one such as she, who couldn't come and go at will? The life of a hybrid offered a tantalizing glimpse of something she'd long dreamed of claiming for herself.

Freedom.

Movement caught her eye. An approaching shadow moving on silent feet—she recognized the action of a born submissive. One of her kind sent to relieve her, at last.

Dipping her head in a show of respect, in spite of how long she'd waited, the girl offered a pleased smile and said, "Matron."

"Omega," the other returned. Addressing the younger female by the title given to those of breeding age. A slur, but one used with affection between those who were born to endure.

Wizened and gray, her bearing years long past, the matron now filled the role of instructor. Tasked to teach the next generation how to please their masters. How to mewl and present so the larger males were not encouraged to damage them too badly or force obedience.

The matron had been preparing her since Hadim had claimed her for his harem. Every three months, when her cycle peaked and her follicles ripened, she was groomed with careful precise fingers. Prepared to submit while she was at her most fertile.

And she was going into heat now.

Her scent cloying, broadcasting her ability to catch Hadim's seed. Warning all other females to stay away or be willing to fight.

"Behave yourself tonight, girl," the matron said, voice pitched low. Intimate. "The master is in a state. Been into the cups with the mistress, I think."

Sneering, the girl rolled her eyes. Her ears flicked back, tail rising in a dark, fluffy arch that signaled her opinion on the matter.

The matron tsked, soothing with a soft touch. "None of that, sweet girl. You know what that temper of yours does to him."

Leaning into her soft palm, the girl dared to soak up the maternal comfort. Eyes drifting closed as unwanted memory burbled to the surface. Bruising fingers. The cut of sharp teeth and cruel words dampened only by the burning stretch of being mounted by a large male utterly unconcerned with the risk of causing damage.

"I hate him," she whispered, voice a frail warbling thing.

The matron took a hiccupping breath, then wrapped her in a squishy embrace. Her cheek pressed to a generous bosom that had nursed dozens—she'd often wondered if this particular matron had been her bearer, or if the other female was just conditioned to be motherly after being forced to birth young she'd not been allowed to raise.

"Submit with grace. Please him as best you can, and I'll have tea brewed and waiting for your return."

Lips quirked in a watery smile, the girl nodded, following the matron to the dressing table.

Experienced enough to know what to expect of the next few days, the girl relaxed as the matron went about preparing her for Hadim. No matter what came next, being pampered was never a thing she could refuse.

For one such as her master—a prince wealthy enough to keep a large harem of breeding Hathorians—the event was little more than a chore.

Rough breeding without the messy Hathorian quirks despised by the Anhur males and their queens alike.

The matron held out a tall, thin glass

filled with milky liquid. "Hurry now, while it's still cold."

Without daring to sniff the offensive offering, the girl set the vial to her lips and threw it back. Swallowed with a grimace, her tongue smacking the roof of her mouth. "Blehhh. Foul shit."

A playful smack bounced off the crown of her head, making her ears twitch. "Don't let the master catch you being so crass."

It was a suppressant designed to ease the symptoms of a Hathorian heat, for when her people went into season, their instincts took over. Without that foul concoction, she'd be driven to build a nest. Mindlessly lifting her tail for a worthy male to catch her scent, to mount her in a nest of her making. And when she was ripe, her sex would glisten with a viscous fluid known as slick.

A lewd, disgusting display unique to her kind. One that had gone out of fashion long before she'd been claimed by a large harem.

Hadim preferred his females tame, their seasons short, litters vast, and their teeth filed down to harmlessly dull Anhur replicas. That he'd left their ears intact wasn't a gesture of kindness, but one meant to highlight their station as slaves.

Her heat cycles were engineered to last three days, though she was really only receptive to male attention for the first two. After her heat had set in, her blood would surge with a potent cocktail of hormones unaffected by the suppressors. Driving her to seek out a dominant male, her mind cluttered with a dense fog unbreakable by anything but time—or a thick, spurting girth of an Anhur male.

Generations of selective breeding had exacerbated that natural trait in the Hathorians, making a new subspecies disinterested in mating with their own males. Unnatural though that might have been, it was no accident. Only the most pleasing females had been selected to pass on their genes, only those who'd been unable to resist their season. Those unable to fight their most basic instincts.

"Sit here, sweets," the matron said, fingers dancing through a section of fine, black hair. "The master requested braids."

Swallowing her vitriol, the girl remained still as her hair was fixed. And when the matron handed her the end of one woven rope, she pinched it in fingers that did not tremble. Even knowing just how Hadim liked to use her braids as leverage, her stoic demeanor was tainted by the hormones flooding her system.

Already, she could feel her attention drifting. Her mind tracing the shape of a tube of lipstick. Recalling the scent of Hadim's sweat after he'd gone into rut to match her season. The heady scent of an aroused male pushing all else to the background. And so she'd remain until the worst of her cycle had passed.

A mindless slit, begging to be filled.

She'd heard the other girls talk of their time with Hadim and knew she didn't have it as bad as some. That she wasn't a favored Omega, her season enviably mild, and her time spent with Hadim reduced to little more than two long days of terse obligation.

The matron handed her a pot of scented oil without making eye contact. And with deft fingers, the girl swirled her first two digits through it, turning her back to discretely slip those fingers inside herself and replace the lubricant she wasn't allowed to produce.

"All set?"

Exhaling a held breath, the girl adjusted her skirts and offered a tight nod. Wishing she could refuse what was coming next.

2

Once more made to stand and wait, the girl fidgeted at the foot of the bed in Hadim's expansive rooms. Her sensitive ears flicking forward and back, her tail tucked out of sight.

The breeding quarters. Separate from the space where he slept, yet close enough to save him the effort of traipsing all the way down to the Harem like a commoner, his females were entombed in a vault.

They went to *him* when they needed to be bred, waited to be serviced, then said thank you before they left. Eyes downcast.

Aching deep in her belly, driven by instinct, she'd come through the private entrance in the eastern corner, following the dimly lit path ascending from the Harem's subterranean rooms. An Anhur tradition, keeping a jealously guarded resource in a vault. Making any who dared to covet such a treasure go through the dominant male himself—and to do that meant a fight to the death, for there was only one way into the Harem. One way out.

Hadim's bedroom.

She'd only ever gone through that door once.

Skin aching with a mild fever, she grew damp but not wet. Needy yet repressed. And no matter the sickly scent of repetitive breeding that hung heavy in the air, the lips of her shorn slit had become sticky with the rush of hormones pumping through her blood.

Heat.

The all-consuming urge to be mounted and stuffed full. To be knotted by an Anhur male, stretched and stimulated until the inflamed gland inside her was compressed. Until it was drained of every last drop of fluid —the swelling forced into submission by a thick knot—she couldn't rest. Couldn't sleep or eat or do much of anything that wouldn't result in being mounted by her captor.

Her master.

The instinct was strong. Unavoidable.

Bred into her kind over a thousand generations to be more pleasing to an Anhur male. More receptive. To take more and take it deeper, she was genetically predisposed to be ready for him at the onset of every new cycle. Her scent modified to emit pheromones utterly irresistible to their masters.

He'd swell first, she knew. Triggered by

her pheromones, his sack would fill with chemicals, pumping truly homicidal levels of testosterone through his blood. In an inexperienced male, that urge would drive him to take a female or die trying. Issuing challenge to any foolish enough to get in the way of his claiming a chance to breed—willing or not. Rejection was merely an obstacle meant to be overcome. Fighting to the death over breeding rights a common, *honorable* way to die.

But in an experienced male like Hadim?

There were no challengers to Hadim's harem.

They were all dead.

His living male siblings were either subservient or uneasy allies, unwilling to challenge the named Heir to the Karahmet throne. Even Hadim's sons were still on the tit, banished, or kept well under thumb.

Guts twisting, the girl fidgeted where she stood. Wishing she could bolt from these rooms and find a male—*any* male—to ease the ache pulsing inside her. Any but the one she'd been promised to since before her birth.

"It's time to let the boys battle for a girl of their own," came a female voice from the hall. "Give them something to distinguish themselves."

The door swung open, revealing Hadim and his wife, both dressed in ceremonial, gold-plated armor. Their hair groomed and doused in scent-neutralizing oils common amongst the upper echelon of Anhur society. Acutely aware of the advantage they had over her, for to disguise their scent—and all that went with it—was to hold power over those who *couldn't.*

Averting her eyes, the girl cringed back from the dominant pair, star-struck by the imposing figure of the statuesque Anhur female Hadim had taken as honored wife.

Samina.

A celebrated warrior, mother of royal bloodlines, and a trusted adviser to the king —she was everything the smaller female wasn't. Everything she'd never dared to hope she could one day be.

An Anhur queen.

"Don't ignore me, Hadim," Samina drawled, slipping out of her over-cloak, tossing thick, sandy hair over her shoulder.

With a snort, Hadim pulled at the laces on his throat piece, discarding it in a careless heap. At ease in his private quarters despite the scantily clad female waiting patiently to be acknowledged.

To be bred.

Stripping off his bracers, Hadim took his time in responding. Head tipped in her direction, just for a moment. And then he scowled at his wife. "Our sons don't need their mother to coddle them soft, Samina. Do you intend to put their cocks in for them too?" He laughed. "If the brats think they're old enough to start collecting a few bitches, they can damn well fight for it. Like I did. Like their grand-sire before me."

Samina shucked her heavy breastplate, cracking her neck with a deep sigh. Beneath the protective layer, the swell of a heavily pregnant female. "I'm not coddling them. They're plenty old enough, my love, and you know it. Besides, if you give them only one between all six, we shall see which has the most promise." She offered a smile, lips teasing and playful where they crinkled at the edges. "You need to name an heir," she said, easing into a plush chair, hands draped over her swollen abdomen. "It's long overdue. Since we lost Sinadim—"

"Enough," he snapped, the stiff ridge of his mane rising up along his spine. But for a moment, Hadim did little more than eye his wife. And shaking himself, said, "Fine. They can have this one when I'm done with her." He discarded the rest of his armor. "Beginning to wonder if she's barren anyway."

Straightening, Samina eyed the girl with keen interest. "Well, isn't that convenient! Lets the boys practice without giving them a proper breeder. No kits running wild underfoot to threaten your position." Humming low in her throat, Samina approached the girl. "She's otherwise capable? Pleasing? Triggers your rut without issue?"

Hadim shrugged, unlacing his pants with his left hand, reaching for the girl with his right. Lips pressed to her cheek, he took a breath of the Hathorian's fine, pale skin, letting her scent fill his brain. "I've been breeding her for a little over three years, and she refuses to take."

"Are your cycles regular, Omega?" Samina asked, her tone not altogether unkind, despite the racial slur.

The girl swallowed and said, "Yes, mistress. Every three months, with the moons."

"Looks healthy enough." Clapping her hands, Samina smiled. "Let's try her on a natural cycle without suppressants, and if she isn't carrying a litter the next time the moons are full, the boys can have her." And then her demeanor shifted. Became almost coy as she glanced at her husband from beneath the fan of thick dark lashes. "Wouldn't want them building an army and challenging their grandfather before you do, hmm?"

Hadim snarled, bristling at his wife's goading insult. His rut beginning to show in earnest. "I will challenge my father when I am ready. On *my* terms, woman." Tail lashing, mane bristling, he turned on her. Fingers tight on the Hathorian female dressed in gossamer silks, he twisted the length of her braids around his fist. A black rope that gave him control over her every terrified breath. "I've got the largest army of all my siblings. Second only to my father himself."

Tail flicking, Samina sashayed away, tossing a sultry, "Yes, well Ahmelek mentioned his intent in passing yesterday. I think he was trying to lure me away from my darling husband," she said, retreating into their marital chambers. "Haven't decided if I'm tempted or not..." Trilling, hearty laughter preceded the soft *click* of her bedroom door sliding shut, having succeeded only in goading Hadim's temper into a seething lather.

Teeth bared, tail whipping and held high, Hadim freed his swollen prick, kneading the base where it bulged. His knot threatening to balloon prematurely. And then, using her braids as leverage, he jerked her closer—then forced her down to her knees.

"Suck," he barked. Still scowling after his wife when he hissed, "Vicious bitch," under his breath.

The girl was inclined to agree. Anhur to her core, Samina had played Hadim's temper, his rut, and his pride to her advantage—and she'd played him *beautifully*. In goading her husband, she'd earned herself a quiet night and a bed free of a rutting male who'd be too tired to bother her when he returned. His energy spent and drained.

Squeezing her eyes shut, the girl bent to her task. Trying not to gag when the tapered tip of Hadim's dick opened her throat. Confident only because she knew he'd soon tire of the accidental scrape of her blunted teeth. That fucking her throat as hard and fast as he wanted would likely result in a corpse that couldn't produce strong hybrids for his army.

Still, he indulged himself. Tugging on his heavy sack with his free hand, kneading as it began to swell. Pausing only long enough to allow her a chance to take a desperate sip of air, before forcing her all the way down once more.

A splash of tangy seed coated her tongue, making her nose wrinkle even as her slit grew plump. Tempted by the salty brine, the *Biquea* glands ringing the inside of her opening grew swollen and ripe, dripping on the luxurious fur rug beneath her knees.

Redoubling her effort to swallow him whole, her mouth watered. Pupils blown wide, her brain filled with the muted scent of a dominant male who could ease the desperate ache throbbing between her thighs.

Rumbling low in his throat, Hadim jerked her off his dick and said, "Up."

Obedient, *almost eager*, the girl assumed the position. Ears following his every movement, her tail flicked high and clear as she braced her hands on the side of the bed.

Hadim kicked her ankles apart and took her tail by its base. Adding pressure, he bent it back, making her mewl in pain even as he forced her down. Face buried in the bedding as she tried to arch away from the dull throb tugging her spine crooked.

The harsh rasp of his stubble whispered between her thighs a millisecond before she felt the caress of a warm tongue. Flicking and probing, he readied her with an air of detached boredom that was still enough to make her gush. A prisoner to instinct, her body responded immediately. Giving him a taste of the hormone-laden lubricant that would send him into rut. One taste of the slick fluid produced by the *Biquea* gland and he'd be primed to fuck her until her cycle ended, keeping her fat and sedate with every copious injection of sperm.

Of course, Hadim would never wholly give himself over to instinct. Would never allow himself to be vulnerable or at the mercy of a female—especially not a Hathorian.

Sparing her nothing, Hadim lined up and seated himself in the oily heat presented before him. Absentmindedly working her tight sheath with a diligent efficiency that saw him thicken to the point of discomfort within a few punishing strokes.

Knowing the male covering her back would finish at exactly the pace that pleased him, she snaked a hand between her thighs. Rubbing furious little circles around the swollen bud of her clit while she still had the sense to do so. Her knuckles grazing his sack with every forward swing.

Some of the courtesans chose to suffer during their heat, punishing themselves, refusing any meager dollop of pleasure a breeding session might bring. But she had long since decided to claim what enjoyment she could in this dreary life, and as Hadim began to bear down, she came.

Fluttering around his girth, she milked him. Powerful internal muscles clenching and pulling, enticing him to go deeper. To lock with her and fill her womb with thick cream and relieve the tension building in her glands.

He denied her even that.

Instead of driving deeper, his strokes turned shallow. And where he should have been fighting to force his knot inside and penetrate that most sacred part of her, she felt it thicken on the wrong side of her sheath. Fucking her with rapid, *shallow* strokes, he held himself back. Knot blooming fat and churlish where it pulsed between her lips. She was left to grasp at his shaft alone. The bundle of nerves within going unstimulated, giving no relief to the persistent ache begging to be stretched out.

With a grunt, he came. Wrenching back on her tail just to make her squirm as he bred her, cruelly refusing to lock with her.

Breath hitching, ears laid flat, she dared to glance over her shoulder. Forgetting herself when she said, "Hadim, *please!*"

He wrenched free of her saturated depths with a breathy snarl, wrapping one large hand about her throat. Mane bristling waves of ruddy brown, his anger pooled between them. His fingers cinching tight enough to choke. With one hand he worked through his orgasm, glazing her asshole, cheeks, and tail in wasted sperm.

And then, lips pressed into the cone of her ear, her tail bent awkwardly against sweat-slicked skin, he hissed, "What did you say?"

Confused, she squirmed against him, left suffering on the edge. Hips lurching back to chase that blissed-out fullness only he could provide. "P-Please, I need—"

His grip about her throat tightened, cutting her off. "You take liberties beyond your station." Hunching, he humped against the curve of her bottom until his tip found her slit once more, then said, "My name is not for your lips."

He was right. Intimate though this act might be, Hadim was not her lover. His name not hers to call out in a moment of foggy passion. "Alpha!" she yelped, scrambling to appease the dominant male at her back with his appropriate title. "Alpha, please, I'm sorry! It was an accident. I didn't mean—I-I wasn't thinking!"

He hauled her arms behind her back and pinned her to the furs, filling her with his shaft as he forced her submission. Knot thick and heaving just outside of her clasping channel. "Allow me to remind you, Omega."

3

Staggering, she made her way through the darkened tunnels. Her every step a concentrated effort, muscles screaming in the agony of one denied time and again. Left to writhe, trying to escape the ants crawling beneath her skin. The twitching, lurching muscles overwrought with lactic acids that had flooded her system when her *Biquea* glands hadn't been stimulated by Hadim's knot.

Her punishment for an insignificant transgression. Two measly syllables spoken at the wrong time.

She stumbled through the dark, all of the torches long since burned down to nothing. The absence of light doing little to hinder her on a path with no turns and only one destination.

The matron was waiting when she finally ambled into the peaceful grotto where the girls were permitted to lounge. Lit with the eerie green glow of an evenwood sapling—a gift from Hadim's father to his most cherished concubine—it was a rare prize indeed. Needing no light to flourish, it fed directly from the nutrient dense soil common in areas with high volcanic activity, giving off light and supporting entire ecosystems beneath its elegant canopy.

"You're back sooner than I thought, dear."

A hiccupping breath escaped chapped lips. The familiar face crinkled at the edges in a welcoming smile that faltered when the girl shuffled into the dim light.

"By the Nine, child! What happened?"

Sobbing, she fell into the squishy embrace, inhaling a breath of comfort from the other female's breasts. And for several long, humiliating minutes of a breakdown, she could do nothing else but vent every emotion she'd ever had. Letting the matron unwind her ruined braids. Massaging at the claw marks scoring her scalp, her hips, the matron ran gnarled fingers through her hair, murmuring against the soft fuzz of her ear.

"Come, darling," the matron said at length. "Tell me what happened?"

Back arching, the girl twisted. Trying to stretch the burn from her limbs, though she already knew it wouldn't work. The only thing that could offer true relief had sent her stumbling from his private rooms. Cock semi-stiff where it hung between his legs, connected to the flesh of his thigh by a strand of sticky, pearlescent drool.

"I..." She swallowed, hard. Eyes downcast, tail tucked tight between trembling legs. "I misspoke and he punished me. Refused to knot."

"Oh, child," the matron clucked, the lines on her forehead deepening around a grimace. "That's cruel indeed. And I'm afraid there's nothing for it but to wait it out, darling. Is this your first time being denied in heat?"

Sniffling, the girl nodded. Her cheeks hot, slick gushing from her aching channel where it saturated the underside of her tail in the cloying scent of spent seed and slick. Unable to deny what she'd been doing with Hadim to a female who'd spent her life doing the same thing.

"Come," the matron continued, setting a pot to boil. "Chances are good that he wasn't able to trigger ovulation without knotting, but you're still fertile, even if he doesn't lock with you. Come and have a nice spot of tea and soak in the spring. The cool water will help with the swelling and muscle spasms."

Mortified, the girl obeyed, for the swelling to which the matron referred wasn't the finger print bruises marking her hips. Nor was it broken blood vessels ringing her throat where Hadim's hands had tightened when he came the last time, choking the girl he refused to knot while he took his pleasure.

No, it was her *Biquea* glands nestled inside her opening, red and glossy. Irritated with a tight, red sheen where they throbbed and oozed, begging for a knot to squash them into submission, trigger ovulation, and end her suffering.

The matron tucked thick calves beneath her, arranging her skirts to conceal the hint of dimpled skin marring her thigh. Fussing, she said, "What did you say to anger him?"

Carefully stepping into the cool, dark water, the girl shivered. Holding her tail high about the surface of the water as long as she could, before sinking down with hitching breath as her genitals were submerged. Unable to deny the relief the cold offered. And then, reluctantly, "His name. He denied me, and I begged for his knot just like he wants. But I said his name."

"Fool girl," the matron hissed, but it was without heat. "My reckless, darling renegade. You're lucky the master chose only to deny you."

"I don't feel lucky," she grumbled, holding herself still in the pool. Trying not to displace the chilly water that had warmed against her skin.

The matron tsked. "None of that. I've seen him beat a girl purple for the same transgression. You will suffer the consequences you earned, child, and be thankful they weren't far worse."

Blunt teeth flashing, the girl turned her

back. Hands dipping between her legs to discretely cleanse her channel of Hadim's seed. To massage her glands with chilly fingers, even though it wouldn't offer relief.

Chuckling, the matron sighed and took a hold of kinky black hair, working to repair her braids. "It'll ease soon enough, dear. And I'm certain you'll not make the same mistake again."

Shivering, yet soothed by the deft fingers gliding through her mussed hair, over the shell of her ears, the girl said, "I won't even think his name."

"I thought not." The matron patted her cheek.

And though couldn't see it, she felt the matron's smile.

For a moment, they sat in companionable silence, broken only by the gentle whisper of water lapping at the edges of the pool and the occasional pitiful sniffle. Each lost in thought. And then, "He's going to give me to his sons. Let them compete and name the winner his heir."

The matron went still. Tension singing in the fine muscles of her hands where they lay against the girl's shoulders. But before she could speak a word of comfort or outrage, the kettle shrilled. Shattering the hush.

With a huff, the matron stood. Turning to fuss with the tea before she returned with a mug of pungent, brackish liquid.

The girl wrapped her fingers around the

warm ceramic with a reluctant nod of thanks. Fingers brushing those that were gnarled and boney. And, lips peeled back in an uncomfortable grimace, she set her lips to the rim and tossed the steaming beverage back in three long gulps. Ignoring the burn of tea that was too hot for comfort in favor of getting it over with.

"Blehhh," she hissed. Gooseflesh pimpling every centimeter of her chilled flesh, she shuddered with disgust. "I'll never get used to that taste."

Rather than respond, the matron placed a soft hand on the girl's cheek. Eyes glistening with emotion. The unspoken sentiment shimmering in milky blue eyes that had faded with age.

Chin dipping, the girl tore her gaze away. Unable to stand the attention, yet grateful all the same. Cherished by her, if no one else.

"Darling"—the matron coughed—"There's something you must understand—"

"Fires of Tor, it's dank and dreary down here!" came the very last voice either Hathorian had expected to hear down in the Harem. "Torches gone out, filth in every corner. I'm going to murder that husband of mine."

Going pale, the matron snatched the empty mug from the girl's fingers and tossed it into the spring. Having only enough time to assume an appropriate pose before Samina herself was standing in the grotto in all her pregnant, Anhur glory. "Mistress, we weren't expecting you. I—you must forgive our lack of preparation."

Samina waved her off. "Nonsense, Omega. How could you have known my husband would be such a colossal ass over so insignificant an error?" She smiled, hands laid over the swell of her distended belly. "I've come to collect the girl. Hadim was rash and cruel to punish her so." Her smile grew sly when she added, "And I was looking forward to a peaceful night with the bed to myself. Come along, girl. Hadim will take care of you because I demand it."

Humbled and in awe, the girl moved to obey. Heedless of the now sheer garment clinging to her nudity, she rose from the bathing pool. Knowing that Samina had seen her in a far more compromising state than she was now. As if in a daze, she went to the Anhur queen. Eager for the burning pain to stop, to be knotted and subdued by Hadim—and by his wife's royal decree, no less.

Blushing to the roots of her pitch-black hair, the girl exhaled a held breath, then said, "Thank you, mistress."

Samina went still, utterly so. Her nostrils flaring wide as she took in the Hathorian's scent, pupils narrow pricks of suspicion. "What is that? What do I smell on your breath?"

The matron fluttered, her hands twisting

restless knots in her skirts. "What smell, mistress? I—"

One hand landing over her belly, Samina took the young Omega by the throat. Pulled her in close, and pressed her nose to against trembling lips. "Breathe," she commanded, loosening her grip.

Tail tucked, ears flat, the girl obeyed without question. A reflex she couldn't help.

It was all Samina needed.

In an instant, her demeanor turned from one of camaraderie to that of a hardened warrior. Stinking of a gravid female protecting her young, Samina's skin grew damp with a fine sheen of sweat. Her tail standing high and proud to broadcast her rage. "Yarrow root. You *dare* to consume that vile filth? *Here*?"

With a pained cry, the matron threw herself at Samina's feet. "She didn't know, mistress! It was all me!"

For a moment, Samina's fingers tightened to the point of pain, making the caught Omega splutter and gag around that clenching grip. And then she threw her to the ground at the matron's side and turned toward the tidy garden at the heart of the grotto. Pausing only long enough to kick over the clay teapot simmering over coals. The expression etched into her proud face was a thing of horrific beauty, the renowned warrior making herself known to the females cowering in the dirt.

With a grunt and only one hand, Samina uprooted the bench, leaving one of the legs mangled and bent before moving on to the rare evenwood tree that needed no sunlight to bloom. Leaving destruction in her wake as she searched for the forbidden flower with its poisonous roots. "Where is it?" she hissed, turning a fearsome glare down the length of her nose.

The matron pointed, soft flesh beneath her arm trembling. Cringing, her ears flicking forward and back a clear sign of her agitation.

And when Samina pulled up the indicated plant in an incriminating shower of dirt, she spun. Her eyes blazing when she snarled, "Up. *Now!*"

Scrambling, the Hathorians did as commanded. Eyes downcast.

"Explain," Samina spat, hurling the Yarrow at their feet.

"It—it was my idea," the matron said again, stammering. Reeking of terrified submission. "I just wanted to give her a few... a few years before she bore Hadim's sons, mistress. A few years without the heartbreak of having a suckling torn from her breast! That's it!"

Samina let out a hissing breath. "Oh, is that it? You eat our food. Enjoy a pampered life bred to a fucking prince, and you dare to insult us by feeding her Yarrow root tea?"

The matron cringed, tail winding tighter between her legs. Ears nearly hidden beneath wiry gray hair. "Only during her heat, mistress, I swear it! She hasn't lost a single litter because they hadn't the chance to implant!"

"Oh, what a comfort to learn you've only been rendering a healthy young breeder infertile!" Samina laughed, incensed. Faster than either Hathorian could react, her hand flashed out and caught the matron by her fleshy upper arm. Stooping until their faces were a few centimeters apart. "Where did you get it, hmm?"

Speechless, the matron's lips parted on a breathless squeak.

"Was it Ahmelek?" Samina asked, deceptively quiet. Taking deep breaths of the matron's scent, her pupils expanding to swallow every last speck of color in her beautiful eyes. A predator readying for a hunt.

The matron could only nod, her fleshy jowls quivering and pale.

"Good," Samina hissed. "I'm going to slaughter that little shit myself."

"I-I beg forgiveness," the matron whispered, staring up at Samina without blinking. "The girl had no part in—"

With a swipe of her claws, Samina lashed out. Seized the matron's windpipe in her left hand, she adjusted her weight and balanced everything on her right foot—placing the left on the matron's chest. And with a snarl, the pregnant Anhur queen pushed and pulled at once.

Too shocked to do more than gape, the

girl watched with wide eyes. Her entire body going slack as the matron's sinew was stretched beyond all hope. Something vital crunched, trapping the matron's screams where her throat bulged. Unheard. And then the skin began to simply... pull apart. Leaving her fat exposed and glistening yellow-white in the gloomy dying glow of the evenwood sapling. Muscles ripping off her spine and jaw with the squelch of torn meat.

Though aged, the matron's frail body had every intention of remaining whole—Samina had to work to claim that fistful of shredded flesh and cartilage.

But it wasn't real.

The horror too vibrant, too *loud* to be anything but a hallucination. A terrible nightmare.

Tendons snapped, leaving thick arteries and veins exposed. Red and blue ropes growing thinner with each passing instant. Pulsing and going pale where the arteries were weakest, tiny little tears began to show through the walls of those rubbery tubes. Misting the air red until they snapped, only seconds apart.

At first, the girl was startled by the color splashing across the bridge of Samina's nose. Almost hypnotized by the beauty of pure crimson. But when the Anhur female fully extended her leg, pressurized streams of gore painted chaos in the air. When blood sprayed hot and sticky across the girl's face—burning her eyes and tinting the world red—she scrambled back at last.

It wasn't far enough.

Limp, the matron fell away from her murderer, a boneless heap making a terrible mess of the grotto. Her head struck the earth with a hollow thud, breath foaming where her voice box should have been. A red lather that spit and hissed and wouldn't stop until the matron's eyes went glassy. Her pupils claiming slow millimeters of watery blue until everything she'd been was nothing more than meat. Empty. Waxy.

The girl choked on a single sob, tasting iron. Gagging when the eyes she'd loved so much rolled, the left one twitching and lurching in the socket. Moving independently of its twin, the right half-hidden behind a hooded eyelid, sightlessly gazing at the ceiling.

Death was ugly. Fucking hideous and wrong.

A whimper burbled up from the girl's chest. Some poor attempt at a eulogy, she could offer those dying eyes no comfort. No parting words of love or a promise to see her again in the arms of the Nine.

She could only see a garish, fleshy mask, drooping where the lips sagged open. Forever slack. A cruel mockery of the kind face that had been smiling only minutes before.

Something crunched and the girl flinched. Scrambling to her feet.

It was Samina.

Nightdress soaked through with blood, her gown clung to her skin. Her distended belly bathed in red, every generous curve of a pregnant female revealed.

It was a grotesque image, but a perfect metaphor for everything that defined the An-hur. Life, born from death.

Samina dropped the chunks of flesh and sinew, letting it splat.

And then she smiled.

4

"**O**mega! Come get this cock, you eager little slut."

The girl shivered, hunkering down into a tiny ball. Trying not to see the hands reaching for her through the steel bars, her tail curled around her thighs in a pathetic bid to shelter from their attention. Shying away from the raspy voices begging her to come closer. To submit and take their bloated girth as deep as they knew she could. It was what she was born and bred for.

"I can smell it on you, Omega," another said, openly jerking off, in spite of the dozen other males in his cage. "You want it, don't you? Come have a taste..."

With a grunt, he came. Spraying fetid cream across the tacky grime coating the floor around her.

And though her heat was easing, her mind clearing of the poisonous hormones that drove her to seek her master, she couldn't help but look. Couldn't help glancing at the ropes of sperm splashed in her direction, her tongue darting out to wet dry lips.

Laughter exploded all around her, the prisoners delighted by her reactionary instinct.

"Can't help herself, poor little breeder." He offered a smile through chipped and blackened teeth. "Daddy has more where that came from, but only if you crawl for it. That's it," he said, eyes gleaming in the dull light. "Lap it all up, and I may just feed you another dose of what you need, baby girl."

Teeth bared, she tucked tighter. Burying her face between her knees, palms pressed to cover her ears. To fold them down and seal them off from the gloomy world around her.

It was dank in her cell. Moist and cold. Unspeakable filth on every surface, but at least she hadn't been thrown in with the males. At least she wouldn't be torn apart between them while fifteen fought over three holes. A small mercy, really, given what she was beginning to understand about herself. About her place on this carnival ride of horrors she'd been born into.

She had hated her life of service to Hadim. Hated being used and bred, talked about as if she weren't capable of speaking for herself. But most of all, she'd hated being kept in the Harem. Unable to see the sunlight, unless she was in Hadim's rooms being fucked silly and knotted placid. Only seeing the sun through a tiny slitted window in the breeding rooms.

But that was before she understood what it was she'd given up. The point not made obvious until she'd been tossed in a prison cell amid a hoard of unattached males, each taking great, woofing breaths of her scent. Prisoners and criminals, sold into the labor forces that kept the Silver City gleaming. Chances were good that she was the only female they'd seen in years—maybe ever, for some of the younger ones had been driven into rut after their first breath of her scent. She'd watched them devolve into savage fucking, shocked speechless as male flesh speared through male flesh. Growing ripe and aroused by the display of flexing and bunching muscles. All that masculine energy clashing and fighting.

And then she was made aware of a startling truth.

Samina had been right.

Life as Hadim's concubine was that of a pampered doll. Under the master, she'd never wanted for food or comfort. An entire harem of Hathorian females were at her disposal. They'd formed a generous sisterhood of support, and without being told, the elder generations lavished their advice upon the younger. Caring for the daughters that weren't theirs, they'd built a community in the dark.

With a single mistake, she'd lost access to a whole quiet culture of Hathorian history.

Her people, now forever out of her reach.

And in that moment, there was nothing she wouldn't have given to take it back. A lifetime of bearing Hadim's hybrids, only to end it teaching the next generation how best to take a thick knot.

She'd been cherished by a bearer with faded blue eyes and sagging dimpled skin.

With a whimper, she squeezed her eyes shut—and recoiled. Assaulted by flashing images of muscles tearing free from tendons. Of flesh with holes growing wider as it was pulled asunder by a merciless grip. Blood whizzing around and around, painting everything crimson. Of one eye rolling until it went white... and the other... the other rolling to stare directly at her.

Accusation gleaming in that faded blue iris.

Feet sticking to the grime, she stood in a rush, letting the muck squelch between her toes.

"That's it, baby girl," the male with black teeth drawled. Straightening when she moved, posturing to catch her attention, his mane standing on end where it wasn't matted to his nape. "Come to Horace."

Sneering, she stalked away, ignoring him. Ears pressed flat to her skull, tail whipping in a fluffy arc at her back. Agitated, she was able to walk a straight-line forward, then back, lest she get too close to either side and get snatched up by grabby fingers.

Instead of ending her, Hadim had given her to the guards at the wall. Banished her from his home, he'd cut her off from everything she'd ever known. The males posted at the wall were... unfit for civilized society. Unable to fight for a harem of their own or simply not given the opportunity. It was the way of things. That so many young males would never know the touch of a female.

Anhur or Hathorian, they were claimed by the strongest warriors. The most promising princes. Hoarded and jealously guarded, no matter their species.

As a consequence, young males were known to form packs, roaming from one hellish living situation to the next. Left with no options, no hope for continuing their lines, they were forced to live together. Surviving on a meager life of crime and the company of their pack brothers.

Most couldn't climb the hierarchy fast enough to escape their end.

It was the fortunate few who were offered a position guarding the wall. Those Anhur rejects were made to watch the fires of the great beyond, as if those who lived in the wilds were capable of scaling the great sloping cliffs.

Hadim and Samina had stood united, hands clasped as they shoved her forward, honoring those who kept their society safe with the gift of a dishonored breeder.

It was an unparalleled gesture. To make a prize of a bloodline such as hers, was an eloquent solution for a unique problem.

That's what he'd called her, when Samina had dragged her back to the master's room, still dripping gore. Still too shocked to speak, much less defend herself, her eyelids sticking together with every blink as the matron's blood grew tacky.

The royal pair had stayed to watch her being mounted, Hadim barking that she be denied a knot while in heat. Made to suffer, so she might be more compliant with the dreary, brutal life she'd been given.

Desperate to please, punished forever.

When they were satisfied their orders would be obeyed, when Hadim and his wife had retreated to their quarters, the girl allowed herself to cry. Cheek pressed to the cold stone atop the wall, her insides being pummeled by the captain of the guard until she succumbed to the bliss of darkness. Waking in her dank little cell, surrounded by criminals.

"Please," one of the younger Anhur males whined, pacing at the edge of the bars. His cock bulging through tattered pants, tail limp and twisted at an awkward angle. "I've never had a female! She smells"—jaws hanging slack, he inhaled, tugging at his prick—"*ss-sooo* good..."

"You wouldn't know what to do with her, runt," snarled another. This one older, his face mangled by hideous scars.

Growing more irate by the instant, the girl hissed, her ears flat. Tail tucked.

"Aww," Horace cooed, working himself hard once more. "Little girl has teeth. Come see if you can use them before I fuck a litter of brats into your belly, hmm?" Grunting, he wedged his cock and balls between the bars. A lewd display that made her ache, nevertheless. Her heat still working its way free of her blood, the instinct lingering. Still poisoning her mind. "What's your name, baby girl? I wanna know what to say when I tell you to take this knot."

But her name would never cross Horace's lips, because she didn't have one. She had a tattoo that bore her lineage. The twisting, elegant designs traced her spine, utterly meaningless to her, but decipherable to the Anhur at a glance. Not knowing that was the mark of an underprivileged male who'd never so much as seen a real harem.

In a flood of sickly torchlight, the prison door banged open, admitting one of the three guards she knew had intimate knowledge of her body—she could still smell his leavings on her skin.

Without a word, he stalked past the cells overflowing with males in rut, threw open her door, and caught her by the nape, saying, "Good morning, Omega."

She didn't bother herself to struggle. Knowing her energy was better spent learning about her new life, knowing the guards would expect a submissive Hathorian, in spite of why Hadim and Samina had rejected her from the harem.

No, instead, she allowed the clawed fist to score her scalp. Eyes watering against her will, taking massive strides to match the gait of the guard driving her up. Toward fresh air not laden with the scent of fluids and horror.

The guard stopped abruptly, pressing her against a damp stone wall. "Hadim commanded us to deny you a knot," he said, forcing a hand between her thighs. Where she was tender and bruised and still sticky. "But once that insufferable cunt is back in his fancy palace, we're going to knot you two at a time." Without warning or grace, fingers speared through her, making her hiss, calves flexing in a futile attempt to wriggle away. "Maybe three, once we've ruined you and this pussy does nothing but gape. Two in this hole, one in your ass."

Heart beating behind her eyes, the girl dared to shrug. "I was born to serve my Alpha."

A toothy grin spread across his lips, making her cheeks hot and damp with a gust of fetid breath. "You are a thirsty little slut, hmm?"

She said nothing, allowing him to play in

fluids that were, for the most part, not her own. Seething.

"I should have come for you earlier," he growled, withdrawing at last. "Could have taken you all night, without any of the others realizing you were gone." At this, he glanced around, checking they were alone. Hesitant, as if he were trying to determine what he could get away with.

And then, "Fuck. There isn't time." He smeared sticky fingers down the front of her ruined harem silks and shoved her forward. A low growl rumbling at her back.

Relieved, she all but ran from him. Knowing this was only the beginning, yet unable to extinguish the fires burning low and sour in her belly.

It wasn't until they stood at the top of the wall, wind ripping through her sheer silks, that the guard released her.

Hadim and Samina were already there. Lounging where they sat in the dull gray morning sunlight. Regal and elegant among the peasants.

"Let's be on with it," Hadim snapped, glowering. "I have duties to attend. Omegas going into heat."

"And a heavily pregnant wife," Samina drawled, reminding him.

The captain of the guard nodded, flustered and stammering. "Of course, my liege. S-sir. My Alpha. The procedure won't take but thirty seconds, once she's been prepared."

Samina scoffed, flicking her wrist. "Then prepare her."

"Mistress," he replied, offering an awkward, misplaced bow. And then, with a steely glint gleaming in storm-gray eyes, he turned to the girl shivering in the wind. Caught her bicep in a hand big enough to almost encircle her waist, then thrust her forward.

She stumbled and tripped, gasping as she fell.

The captain was on her before her palms touched the stone. Hauling her up, he bent her over a strange bench. Placing her head and wrists before trapping her there with a wooden panel that pressed against the back of her thighs—another clapped shut around the back of her neck. Locking her in place with a snap that forced a whine between her lips.

A modified stock. He'd bound her in a fucking stock! Hands frozen on either side of her face, left exposed, vulnerable and utterly unable to defend herself.

It was only when the first sounds of panic began to bubble past her lips that Hadim bothered himself to stand. Only then, when she could do nothing but watch him approach, did he deign to address her.

"You're being punished, Omega," he whispered, stroking her hair back with fingers that had touched every single millimeter of her skin. Inside and out. "It wasn't enough to send you here. To know you'd spend the rest of your miserable life shitting out peasant brats. Whelping them by the dozens." His lips curved, mimicking a smile. "No, I want you open and exposed at all times. Nothing between your treacherous cunt and whoever wants to stretch you out." Teeth bared, he pressed in. Lips grazing the shell of her ear. "You're going to spend the rest of your life marked. Like the filthy little criminal you are."

She couldn't make a sound. Jaws hanging slack, sweat blooming on her skin.

And then she felt a hand slipping between her thigh and the wooden panel keeping her over that bench. A searching, wriggling hand that was both utilitarian, and far, *far* too intimate. Her skirt was hauled up first, leaving her cheeks bare to kiss the smooth surface of the wood, her tail wedging tighter between the naked lips of her pussy.

It wasn't enough. Rough fingers dove between her cheeks, jabbing without care at delicate tissue. Fingernails chewed short and ragged made her flinch. But it didn't last— not when he managed to hook one finger between her asshole and her tail, then pulled, dragging that fifth limb over the edge of the wood. Stopping her from struggling when he caught it in the heart of his palm, right at the base, and twisted. Making her spine kink and another piteous cry spill between her lips.

"Please!" she shrieked, not knowing exactly what to beg for. Knowing mercy was not an option, but begging nevertheless.

The captain leaned over her, producing another plank of wood from outside her limited range of vision. He set it beneath her raised tail, pushing until it felt like he'd jammed the entire thing up her ass sideways. Until it clicked into place, forming a working ledge under her tail.

"By the flames, *no*," she whispered, horrified tears streaming unchecked down her face. Her ears aching with the unconscious effort to keep them laid back.

"Water," the captain said, and grunted seconds before liquid ice splashed over her lower back. Soaking the thick, black fur of her tail.

She yelped, bucking in place.

"Easy, Omega," he murmured, not unkind. "It'll be over soon."

The scent of astringent stung her nostrils, feeding the flames of panic when it landed on her tail. Burning her ass when she felt him saturate her fur with foaming cream. "Please, *please!*"

A blade landed on her lower back, where her tail met her cheeks. And then, with short, grating strokes, the captain began to shave her. Nicking the skin with every rusty scrape along flesh that was thin enough to see the shape of the bone beneath. Leaving her tail naked and bleeding at the base, he ignored the rest of her glorious black and gray fur.

"What's this?" Samina asked, approaching. Her head tilted to the side, curiosity etched across her beautiful face. "Why bother shaving her?"

"Dulls the blade," the captain replied, gruff. "Unless you want her crippled, it must be a clean strike."

Sobbing now, she met Hadim's gaze and saw her doom. The delight as he glutted himself, drinking in every helpless instant of her anguish until she could smell that the rut was upon him once more. Unprompted by the scent of breeding females, this was bloodlust. What an Anhur really was, beneath it all.

"Oh, no," Hadim said, gesturing for the other male to continue preparing her. "I want her to feel every moment of this, for the rest of her life."

Cold steel clamped around the base of her tail, making her bleed anew where it pinched the skin. Tight enough to cut off the blood supply and compress nerves.

"Alpha, *please!* I didn't know what the tea was! That it was making me barren! You must believe me," she cried, voice cracking as she babbled, snot running freely over her lip. And yet, Hadim seemed to consider it, his eyes narrowed as if in thought. "Every time my courses ran, my heart broke," she said, almost giddy that he'd let her continue, that she might actually have a chance of convincing him not to do this. "I want nothing more than to please you, my Alpha.

Anything, *anything* you want, I will give you if I can. I-I had no idea the matron was capable of doing something so... so... *vile*. I would kill her myself, if the mistress hadn't done such an—" her voice failed her when her breath ran short, and she gasped in a quick lungful without pause—"an efficient job of it."

Hadim hummed, inspecting her lips. Her eyes, and the quivering shell of her ears. Almost... caressing her with a contemplative gaze. And then he nodded, capturing her lip with his thumb.

A hysterical laugh burbled up. "Oh, thank you, Alpha. Thank you." She returned his smile, trying to radiate a false love. Relief making her shiver, fresh tears spilling over her lashes. "I promise—"

"No."

She blinked. "A-Alpha?"

That smile grew pointed... sharp. "No," he said again, enunciating as he stood, adjusting an impressive bulge distorting the front of his pants. "I don't believe you, and I won't have a breeder I can't trust. No matter her prized lineage."

"What—" she stopped, choking on confusion until she saw the look on Samina's face. Felt the burn of pure hatred where it seared her skin. And then she understood how deadly a thing hope could be when it was given only to be ripped away.

"Go ahead, Captain Grier," Hadim said,

kissing his wife's cheek. Caressing the swell of their next litter of Anhur babes.

"No!" she shrieked, jerking and thrashing until her every muscle ached. Bruises promising to bloom where she was bound.

The blade whistled as it fell.

5

A dull throb spiked through her nerves. The shock of loss the only thing that kept her from feeling the trauma. The truth.

That she'd been docked.

Her glorious fifth limb of black, fluffy fur was gone, though she could still feel it flexing and twisting at her back. Could still tuck it between her cheeks and hide from the cold inspection of the Anhur gathered at her back, if only she could concentrate hard enough.

"Was it a success?" Samina asked, hushed. Her tone holding a note of reverent respect, in spite of the terrible thing she'd just ordered done.

Hadim chuckled as he said, "Can you feel this, Omega?" then proceeded to prod the fresh wound.

The girl howled, bucking against the wooden stocks as lightning blasted up her ass.

"A fine job, Captain Grier," Hadim said, digging his finger in, scraping at the severed nerve of her stump.

Sobbing, she began to shiver. Sweat soaking her hair faster than the wind could dry it. She felt the blood drain from her face with each fluttery beat of her heart, the shock setting in and making her ill, even as it dulled the majority of the pain. Pain she knew would come roaring back the instant her adrenal glands gave up the fight.

But that was *nothing* in comparison to the shock of losing something so precious.

Even so... Hadim didn't stop until she was heaving in her bonds. Thrashing when his fingernail caught the jagged edge of exposed vertebrae, she puked up stringy yellow bile in the absence of substantial food, utterly unable to beg for relief or simply draw breath.

Hadim was far from finished, and though he abandoned her stump with a hearty chuckle, he rounded the stocks and knelt before her once more. Waiting until she'd caught her breath before saying, "A parting gift, Omega. The symbol of what you'll be, forever." And with that, he pried her fingers apart, wrapping them around a cold, bony rope.

Her tail.

Severed, the black fur remained luxurious despite the blood. Beautiful, no matter that it was inert. That it twitched between her fingers and died in her hands. The nerves starved of oxygen with each passing second.

A low keening erupted from her lips, sorrow spilling forth unfettered. Her fingers clenching around that which was no longer hers, unable to let go or admit it had really happened at all. But still, she sobbed until something popped in her eye. A blood vessel, perhaps. Her voice hoarse and ragged as she choked and gagged and sobbed.

She heard words directed at her seconds before warm liquid dripped into the open wound, stinging viciously enough that she was shaken from her misery and tossed into torment.

"Take another breath for me now, Omega," the captain of the guard murmured, shushing her. Quick fingers working to clean her stump.

"No painkillers," Hadim drawled, and stroked at the tears tracking down her cheeks. "Not for her."

She blinked, tears running hot and fresh down her cheeks. Pain radiating from what was now the base of her spine, tingling with an antiseptic burn.

"Will you trim her ears?" Hadim asked, tugging at the expressive feature. The very last of her Hathorian pride left up to the whim of her new owner.

The captain cleared his throat, uncomfortable, but saying, "If it's up to me, I'd rather not, sir. Better to be reminded of what she is, and I'm fond of the look."

Hadim shrugged, giving one final, cruel tug before he stood.

"Come, my love," Samina said, gathering her shawl tighter about her shoulders. "It's a long trek home."

Hadim nodded, licking his lips. Eyes glinting with a sharp, predatory edge. And then, to the captain of the guard, "She'll give you many strong hybrids to serve at the wall, as long as you breed her regularly. And," he added, clapping a bit of loose black fur from his palms, "might I recommend breeding her to as many of your soldiers as possible?" He laughed, kissing Samina's cheek. "By the fires, why not let a few of the prisoners at her? Use her as a reward for good behavior."

A pitiful little sound burbled between her lips. Scarcely a whisper, but all she had left.

The captain worked at the stock, lifting the brace keeping her neck and hands locked down. His touch gentle, even daring to stroke her nape when she whimpered. Almost as if... as if he pitied her, for what he'd done.

What he'd been made to do.

It wasn't until she'd been freed that she was able to control her sniffling. That she could stand to meet the eyes of the Anhur monsters who'd maimed her, still clutching her severed limb in both hands.

Hadim smiled. Gloating, even then.

"Let's be going, love," Samina said, looking away.

Scrambling, the captain bowed to the royal pair. One hand pressed to his heart, the other crossed over his waist—leaving the girl shivering unsupported. Unchained. "Thank you for this treasure, my prince. We will honor your wishes, and she will give us many strong soldiers to protect the Silver City."

Hadim flicked his wrist, bored now that the day's entertainment had ended. "Yes, see that she does."

Clutching her tail to her breast, she dared to scowl at his back. Fur matted with blood, sticking to her fingers as she held her severed limb in a ginger grip. As if it wasn't real, so long as she didn't feel the way delicate bones poked through thin skin. Didn't feel the occasional spasm of dying nerves, or that she was tipped too far forward. Over compensating for the loss of a thing she'd learned to walk with.

But it had happened. She'd been docked. It was the ultimate shame, the mark of a criminal. Outcast.

A renegade.

Off balance, she wobbled in the chill, light headed and in shock. Watching as the captain debased himself before the royal pair, his back turned.

Gaze wandering to the wall and beyond, she stroked at the black fur she'd once groomed to catch Hadim's attention. Inspecting the void on the other side. The empty expanse of sky shining blue and pristine. An insulting contrast, and one that made her lips curl in a watery sneer.

The decision was easy.

The opportunity ripe.

And without pausing to over-think, the girl seized her moment. Took advantage of the captain's lapse in attention and turned on the spot. Fled, despite the pain and her center of gravity being pitched forward. Pouring everything she had into the perfect escape, she ignored the agony splintering through her nervous system. She lifted her feet high, so her toes wouldn't drag. So any stumble would be minor as her strides grew longer with every shouted command for her to, "*Stop!* Omega, stop!" Footsteps at her back making her heart lurch, her window snapping shut, almost out of reach.

When her left foot landed on the stone railing, her elbow was caught in a bruising grip. His fingers long enough to set the tips of his claws into her armpit. And though she had enough momentum to carry her over, she was stopped short—held teetering over the edge. Stalled.

Snarling, she whirled again, this time turning to meet the vicious male that had ruined her.

Hadim. His mane standing rigid, clawed

grip leaving deep gouges in the muscle where he'd caught her.

But the decision she'd made was not one to be easily unmade, and with a nasty smile perched on her lips, the girl took a swing. Lashing out with her free hand, she punched her master in the throat.

The sound he made was nearly gratifying enough to make her do it again. A strangled squawk she'd never heard an Anhur make, let alone one like Hadim. A named prince. Recognized heir to the Karahmet throne. It was enough that his grip faltered. That he let her teeter toward oblivion as he hacked and coughed, red in the face.

Going rigid, she let the weight of her body carry her over. And as she slipped free of Hadim's grip, the slender muscle of her bicep was scored from armpit to wrist.

Coughing, his hand darted out, eyes ablaze with outrage. Halting her fall with the hand not clutching at a bruised windpipe.

But he missed her wrist entirely.

Instead, his fingers caught at that severed limb. Her tail. The shaved and bleeding end clutched in her fist, the fluffy black tip clenched in his. Crunching when he tried to yank her back, she watched the end lurch to the right. The vertebrae dislocated, forever kinked—and she didn't feel even a whisper of phantom pain, though the sight of it made her sick. Queasy with a sour, out-of-body sensation to see her tail separate from herself. Now broken and bent.

Held frozen in a tableau—her weight suspended over the void beyond the wall—Hadim was unable to move, lest he shatter the delicate balance that held her still.

"Omega, *come*," he said, issuing command in a voice that had once made her quiver with the need to submit.

Now absent.

Instead of desperate obedience, a brief flare of seething contempt, then... nothing.

She glanced down, to the thousand-foot drop separating the Silver City from the wilds of the great beyond.

"Omega," Hadim growled, and tugged on his end of their ghastly life-line. His voice hoarse and raspy.

She met his glare. Saw the malice simmering behind a thin veneer of civility and knew it to be a lie. What looked to be meek was merely waiting for a chance to strike. Poorly disguised beneath a thin and tattered cloak, a monster waited. One that would *never* abide her abhorrent behavior. That she'd dared to strike him.

A smile creased her lips—the first that had ever done so.

And it was beautiful, stripping years of torment off her skin in a single instant.

Hadim had taken much. Everything he could.

But not this.

Still smiling, she simply... let go. Her stomach lurched, the wind roaring in her ears as she began the free fall toward the only truly independent decision she'd ever made.

She'd always wondered what it was to fly.

<h1 style="text-align:center">6</h1>

She was falling.

The wind screaming in her ears as Hadim's shocked face grew tiny and distant, her tail still locked in his grip as he stared over the edge of the wall. Watching her escape his claws for good.

Death would be ugly for her—she'd always known that truth—but at least it wasn't the life of a dishonored royal concubine sentenced to breed for the cretins doomed at the wall.

She tried to relax, letting the wind take her remaining limbs and whip them around. It wouldn't be long, now. Not long at all, given just how fast she was plummeting toward the ground.

But when she felt the impact, it wasn't the world-ending thump it should have been.

At first, all she felt was the sting of rock kissing skin. The nip of her elbows sliding along the sheer face of the wall, happening too fast to be anything but irritating. Maybe a little shocking. Too fast for the pain to register, certainly. It wasn't until she physically struck an outcropping that she was spun around. Not until she was forced to really see that she understood.

The base of the wall was sloped stone, polished by a thousand years of exposure to the elements.

A giant slide, ending in what was once a moat.

Now facing her doom, she was treated to the sight of the ground rushing toward her. Of the thousands upon thousands of bodies that lay broken at the bottom, crippled by the fall. Left to die in slow agony. Alone.

By the fires, *what had she done?*

Flailing, she screamed louder than the wind. At the top of her lungs, until she collided with the wall once more. Her jagged tail bone took the brunt of the impact, laid her out flat in a great *oomph* of stolen breath and dazed vision.

She was spinning out of control. Rolling, now. Knees, elbows, and hips taking on the chore of slowing her down as she curled around herself and tried to bear it. Elbows skinned to the bone in a single instant of contact with stone.

But still, she fell. Arms wrapped around her face, she tumbled. Bounced twice. The pitch growing less and less severe as the seconds rushed by, her speed reduced until she no longer had the momentum to spin. Instead, she slid. Feet first. Her obliterated harem silks nothing more than scraps that had bunched around her hips. Offering the slightest amount of protection against the very real danger of being skinned alive before she could find release from her torment.

When the wall began to level out, she knew she'd failed. Her great escape botched by an optical illusion not visible from a thousand feet above. And now, a greater danger than splattering on the stones below.

Bodies.

A great trench that had once held a moat stocked with vicious water dwellers, was now nothing more than a great slide littered with the bones of the less fortunate—bones that were jagged and broken. Glaring white.

The first one she struck merely glanced off her foot. Whizzing past her face so fast she hadn't a clue what it might have once been, only that it hadn't been living for too many seasons to count.

She screamed again, trying to plant her feet. To slow herself before she was bisected and impaled by a shattered femur.

But it was no use. The only result? Raw and burning feet.

Still, she had to try. Couldn't just accept so gruesome a fate, no matter that she'd decided to end it.

Her feet caught on a clump of old clothing, the sudden friction launching her upright in an instant. Windmilling, she scrambled for balance as her legs pumped. Running wildly. Moving so fast she felt something pull in her back, but though she was indeed slowing, it was impossible to stop until gravity had finished toying with her.

Staggering, she tripped. Feet tangling in something that squished, she went down. Tucking her arms and legs, she was thrown end over end, tumbling with a squeal of pain that belittled just how fantastic her fall had been. How... comically unlikely to fall a thousand feet and survive. She didn't stop until she collided with the last unfortunate soul to meet his end over the wall.

The body split open upon impact. Intestines bursting out the other side of the abdomen, she unleashed an unholy stench as foul liquid seeped into her open wounds. Gasping, she lurched to her feet and swayed on the spot. Disoriented. Shaking.

A narrow channel of brackish water was all that remained of the moat, and she focused on that, ignoring the reek of rotting flesh baking in the early morning sun.

There were flowers. Elegant, billowing petals speckled with electric purple that sparkled and danced. Waving in a gentle breeze.

She exhaled a shuddering breath and took a step. The tiny movement sending a shock of pain rattling through her bones. Every millimeter of skin aching and burning, throbbing with every lurching pulse of her heart.

"Fuck," she gasped, clutching at her throat. "*Fuck!*"

With a strangled cry, she made her way to the water. Unbalanced. Stepping over bits of the corpse and all the others beyond. A literal graveyard of criminals and rejects sent to die beyond the wall. Some were little more than skeletons, almost powdered by age, while others still were mummified husks. The worst were the fresh ones. Like the massive hybrid who'd been thin to the point of emaciation before he'd fallen, his skin still sweating putrefied fat.

She retched, the heaves making the damaged skin of her back split and bleed anew, but she pressed on. Eyes focused on the pretty white and purple flowers beckoning from the stream, and not what oozed between her toes.

When she was able to navigate to the edge of the moat, she fell to her knees. Voice splintering when open wounds landed in muck, but unable to do much else but endure.

For a time, she merely stared into her reflection, on all fours. Gasping and shaking as the waters were stained red, her mind befuddled by the shock of it all.

Would Hadim come for her now? Would he make the trek down just to see if she'd done the impossible and survived? And if *she'd* lived, surely... surely she wasn't the only one? There must be others.

Males.

Criminals, starved for female attention. Those who'd do worse than Hadim on their best day.

She swallowed. Bracing to stand, for she couldn't stay.

No, for better or much, *much* worse, she was beyond the wall. The Nine had granted her the chance to live free, just as she'd wished. Transaction complete, her freedom bought and paid for in blood, slick, and tears. Just there, on the other side of the narrow moat, lay the wilds in all their untamed glory.

But she was just a harem girl, and not a very good one at that. She'd been called a renegade for her inability to adapt or submit to the life of a pet. How could she possibly survive on her own?

A breathless laugh burst from her lips. Wasn't this freedom? The right to fail at her leisure? To make her own decisions and do exactly as she pleased? Even if it meant an ugly death.

Taking another breath, she caught her own gaze, willing herself to find the strength to stand. The eyes staring back at her reflected the sun through murky water, blazing an angry yellow.

Swaying, the flower caught her attention as it danced in the breeze. Petals shimmering, the scent of honeysuckle thick and cloying. Making her mouth water.

Ears sagging and relaxed, she reached for it. A loopy grin distorting her lips as she stretched, fully extended over the surface.

A gust of wind pushed her hair back— but the flower remained fixed and rigid. Unnaturally so.

Head tilting to the side, she frowned. And, fingers frozen mere millimeters from touching it, she glanced down and met the eyes of her reflection.

Yellow, angry eyes. Elongated pupils that stood tall and slitted.

Alien.

With a gasp, she scrambled back just in time.

The flower straightened, then was sucked out of sight.

A great yawning mouth snapped open beneath the surface, leaving a void that splashed when it fell. And before that cavernous maw could close, she stared into a creature that could swallow her whole. An oblong disk, it lurked unseen, mostly flat. Disguised in less than a foot of water, this predator would simply wait until some hapless idiot was ensnared by a pretty dancing flower. Lured by the scent of finer things.

Water gushing everywhere, its jaw flapped shut, filtering the excess liquid through gill slits that ran along the visible part of its body. Geysers filtering what might have been her grave.

Overwhelmed, the girl laughed as she stood once more. Teetering toward hysterics, she embraced false security, presuming the creature was not land worthy with so ungainly a body, and turned from the water's edge. Giving up her back, she set her gaze to the field of bodies and everything on her side of the moat.

Concrete, bones, and death. Nothing more, except the vague possibility that Hadim might be coming for her. The stark knowledge that no matter how much she hurt or bled, no matter the urge to lay down and sleep forever, *she could not stay.*

And so, with gritted teeth and throbbing tail bone, she pressed on. Searching for valuables amongst the dead, ignoring the worst of her wounds.

It wasn't long before she was outfitted in leathers that hung from her slender frame, a backpack stuffed full of various other scavenged goods slung over the shoulder less damaged from her fall. Her wounds throbbing and screaming for relief, but the girl knew she couldn't stop. Not until she'd devised some way over the moat. Not until the wall was out of sight and Hadim nothing more than a recurring nightmare.

Her eye caught on his banner—a red lavakin on black silk—flapping in the breeze. Threatening and ominous, for it was attached to a spear. A spear that could only have been thrown from the wall above, impaling some unfortunate that had died many seasons past.

But to the girl, it was salvation.

Scrambling over a pile of bones, she climbed until she reached the summit. Retrieved the spear and finally returned her attention to the moat.

Her timing would have to be flawless, or it was all for nothing. Her unsteady balance compensated for. One shot, or she'd learn what was inside those ugly water dwellers that could swallow an Anhur whole.

Balanced on the edge of the moat, she approached the nearest flower. Scanning for gleaming yellow eyes.

It was a stupid beast. One that would try the same tactic over and over, until its hunger was sated. But it was that same lack of intelligence that served her so well, and with a deep breath, she found her balance. Took aim, then lunged.

The spear landed beautifully. With a heavy *thunk* that struck between the eyes. But she did not release her weapon, instead redoubling her grip, she leapt. Feet landing on the beast's slippery skin, toes finding purchase in the gill slits, she clung to the spear's shaft. Squealing at the top of her scratchy voice.

Already dying, the predator reared and took her with it. Spinning, it thrashed, lifting her and the spear into the air as it whirled.

Flooding the banks. Displacing a tsunami that swept bodies by the dozen into the murky water.

But as it lurched away from the pain pounding into its primitive brain, it ferried her to the other side. Legs hanging perpendicular to the damp ground, her fingers clutching the spear with every last remaining ounce of strength, she simply... stepped off on the opposite bank. Making sure to yank her spear from the flesh before she went.

It was then, as she plopped down into the muddy bank with the wilds at her back, that she took notice of a much larger beast. In less time than it took her to blink, a void opened up beneath her boatman, and it slid into the gullet of a creature so large, it shouldn't have been able to exist in water so shallow.

Smearing the muck from her hands down her thighs, she stood. Dressed in scavenged leathers, knowing she stank of death, the girl dared to smile—and it was terrible.

7

Pressing her face deeper into the thin blanket of fur, she scowled and kicked. Uncomfortable. Sweating hot, yet unwilling to sleep in the nude, lest some uninvited guest stumble into the cave she'd chosen for the night. Her spear clenched between calloused fingers. For months, she'd been able to scrape by undetected, relying on the utterly foul scent that saturated her leathers.

Dead man's fat.

It clung like nothing else. Saturated her scent with that of carrion and made her invisible to the males who roamed these woods.

And the monsters.

But if it was wearing off?

Shivering in spite of the heat, she threw off her blanket. She'd have to find another corpse.

"Should have tried to collect some off the last dead Anhur," she mumbled, yawning.

Speaking aloud just to hear another voice, to break the silence so it matched her mood. For the third night in a row, sleep had evaded and mocked, leaving her skin hot and itchy. Her eyes burning, aching and light-sensitive.

Bleary-eyed, she stumbled over loose shale and into the moonlight, her spear doubling as a walking staff. The stub of her docked tail sending splinters of pain shooting through her nerves with every other step—a sensation she'd grown accustomed to, no matter how irritating.

Three times, the moons had waned.

Three times they'd waxed while she'd been living this new life of a renegade.

Teeth flashing, she shook out sweat damp hair, gazing up at the triplet moons. Her skin cooling in a gentle breeze. It was a hard life, but one she relished. She'd *survived*. Eaten her first kill raw and done her best to learn the old witching ways. Teaching herself to eat from the forest, where to find the best shelter, and the water not poisoned with volcanic sulfur. That it was best to hide from the vicious beasts dominating the wild.

She'd seen creatures beyond anything she could possibly imagine. A flock of tiny jewel colored, winged lizards that spit acid and gorged on scalded flesh. Giant, tusked water wallowers caked in decades of muck, a veritable island of mud and vegetation growing straight from their broad, oblong backs.

And she'd taken pains not to be seen by

the packs of roaming predators. Those stealthy jungle lurkers who stalked the edge of the visible world. Ravenous. Dressed in claws and teeth and poisoned barbs, their senses attuned to the dark. Their appetites bottomless, outmatched only by the next hungry mouth fighting for supremacy.

The wilds suffered no innocent fools.

She grew hardened by all that she saw, felt something akin to sympathy for the An-hur, who'd come from this hellscape of volcanic misery. For those ancient tribal packs who'd needed to fight for every breath, made to evolve simply to survive deadly herbivores and demonic predators.

But she would never forget Hadim. That he might be coming for her, even now. Bent on retribution, on punishing her until the very last breath was forced from her lungs.

So she learned to avoid detection from those who would enslave.

It was vigilance and experimentation, pure and simple.

When another might be content to find a place to stay, she roamed. Never sleeping in the same den twice, she hunted when her stomach growled. Mastered the spear that had kept her alive and ate her fill of the forest's bounty. Utterly lawless, she'd found the life that suited her best.

Where once she'd been all soft curves and delicate angles, she was now hard and lean. Coated in rangy muscle, her body could meet the challenge and demand she required of it.

She was *happy*, living this life of an outcast. For the first time ever.

Days away from the nearest civilization, she'd wandered as far as she could, always away from Hadim, to the outskirts of any conquered lands just to see what she could see. And with each passing day, she grew to hate where she'd come from. Hated everything about the Silver City, where the Anhur clung to their shiny technology and insufferable rules. Cowering behind a wall that kept them safe from what lurked in the untamed wilds.

It was the Trax virus that had driven those ancient conquerors to form alliances, to share resources and bind together in the safety of numbers.

No longer a valid threat, as far as she was concerned, for she'd been living in the beyond for months without so much as coming down with a cough.

Collecting her spear, she settled into the insomnia, sharpening the tip and refastening the ties. Her gear was far from pristine, but it was arguably the best cared for on this side of the wall, for she and the night were fast becoming lovers. In the absence of sleep, she filled the small hours with busy work to keep her mind off the aching solitude.

It was rarely enough.

When the spear was as sharp as it'd ever be, she set it aside, stretching to dispel the memories that clung to her nape and soured an already delicate mood. Wide awake as the sky began to lighten. Morning's sunlight making the very air grow damp. Moist and oppressive.

Still, she gathered her frayed nerves, stripped off her jacket, and strolled along the forest's edge. Looking for edibles and whatever else she could scavenge, hoping to spend her excess energy and earn a few hours of honest rest before she moved on.

Stooping, she prodded at a patch of spongy moss and found it delightful to the touch. Dense, without being hard—soft, but not wet.

Perfect.

Alert, even as she pocketed the moss, she kept her senses sharp. Attuned to the quiet sounds of early morning, listening for anything out of place. For the whistle of the winged lizards as they descended with the intent to feast, and the thrumping groans of the grazers as they chewed their cud.

A sparkle caught her eye. The glitter of pink quartz trapped in a dull gray stone. It would be stunning in the sunlight.

She smiled as she claimed it. Turning it over and over in her hands, already thinking of the perfect place for the semiprecious stone, she tucked it away.

And so she continued, foraging for flotsam, stuffing her pockets to bursting.

The sun was hot overhead when she finally staggered back to her den. Exhausted and sore. Collapsing, she wrapped herself in a patchy fur blanket, one she'd managed to craft from the pelt of her first kill. Eyelids heavy.

But no matter how hard she tried, nor how bruised her muscles, sleep would not come.

Back aching, she tossed.

Skin hot and damp, she turned.

Uncomfortable.

"*Fuck*," she hissed, and stripped off her jacket, bunching it beneath her head in the rough shape of a pillow. Breaking her personal rules in a fit of irritation, she was met with the ugly scars Hadim had left on her right arm. The raised edges still swollen and shiny with regrowth.

The pants went next, and for the first time since she'd been living in the wilds, she was nude.

And it was fucking *divine*.

"By the fires..." She groaned, shivering not because of the cool breeze caressing her skin, but the pure luxury of sensation. Smooth as silk, the inside of the pelt glided over her back. An all-encompassing hug when she snuggled deeper, wrapped herself in tighter.

She slept for a time, and it was dreamless. The sleep of the truly exhausted, she didn't move for the better half of an hour. Didn't so much as twitch or squirm.

Until the ache returned to her muscles. The frown between her brows growing deep. Ugly.

Her wrist *ached*. Throbbing, she flexed and twisted. Trying to shake the pain away.

A splintered moan leaked from her lips seconds before she was crawling from her bedding. Groggy. Disoriented. With her eyes squeezed shut, she began to pick through her meager supplies. Scouring through the things she'd gathered from the forest, she stopped only when her fingers came across something soft. Spongy without being wet.

She cooed high at the back of her throat, a soft smile stretching her lips. Thighs gliding together as she crawled back to her bed, placing the bit of moss *just so,* beneath the back of her left wrist. She adjusted it over and over and over again, until she found the perfect angle. Exhaling a gusty breath of relief.

But it didn't last.

The ache had seeped into the meat of her thigh, but she had the perfect thing for it...

It wasn't until she was surrounded by a heap of various forest fluffs, her ears twitching restlessly, that she began to suspect. Not until the sun had already set that she grew suspicious of the pleasant hum of a job well done.

Cold sweat seeped into her hairline as realization dawned. Trembling, she moved the collection of feathers balanced over her forearm, fingers traveling down. Skating over the leaves speckling her hips, the blanket folded at precise right angles, and the legs of her pants.

Soaked.

Her pussy was swollen and wet, thighs slippery with lubricant. And worse, it was the sort of wet only a Hathorian could produce. That she'd never seen it before didn't change the instant recognition.

Slick.

More viscous than her usual fluids, it was the mark of one born to serve, a walking womb meant to carry the next generation of soldiers. A lure for the dominant species that had turned her kind into incubators.

Forced evolution had cursed her kind to a lifetime on her back, legs splayed as copious fluids leaked out. Stuffed and sealed by whichever male proved himself worthy of breeding rights. Not even an Anhur female could endure a true rut like an Omega could, for slick offered great endurance, even as it punished. Blurred the lines between pain and pleasure.

Where others would tear, slick gave a rutting Anhur male easy passage.

The girl moaned, playing in the wetness between her thighs. Oozing between her fingers.

Hadim had hated the mess. All the harem girls had been made to take vitamins and suppressors to keep their hormones from spiking out of control and ruining the bedsheets.

And as she glanced around at the thing she'd made, she began to understand what she'd done without realizing.

A nest.

Made in the absence of proper building supplies, perhaps, but it was recognizable nevertheless. The first she'd ever made, it was a shoddy thing dredged from ancient memory. Crafted entirely from detritus from the forest floor, and yet, she couldn't deny the comfort it offered now that her nest was complete. That the wandering ache had left her in peace at last.

She scrambled free, kicking and thrashing until the nest was little more than scattered garbage. Ruined, but not beyond repair.

If she was nesting, that could only mean one thing—she was going into season.

Her first, terrifying, unmanaged heat without Hadim's knot to see her through. Without the suppressors to keep her hormones in check.

Shaking, she dropped to her knees, an ache bunched between her shoulder blades... fingers itching to rebuild her nest...

8

Heat.

It throbbed and twitched, oozing through her blood. Overpowering the scent of dead man's fat, she reeked of fertility. Her scent promising this to be the most intense season she'd ever weathered.

Without suppressors. Without Hadim's thick knot to force her submission.

Ears going flat, she hissed, baring her blunted teeth. Seeing her master's hated face every time she blinked. Remembering his scent, the taste of his seed. And with each beat of her heart, the throb of her stump fed the well of seething hatred simmering in her gut.

But still, she ached for the only cock that had ever offered relief. For the knot that had torn through her maidenhead and shaped her to thrive on violence.

Already, the *Biquea* glands inside her

sodden channel were pulsing and swollen with hormones. Begging for release, making her mindless with hunger. Thirsty for a spurting prick to fill her to overflowing.

Hands shaking, she put bone knife to the hilt of her spear.

What need had *she* of Hadim? She, who ate when she hungered, who wandered at her leisure. Making it through a heat without her master should be *easy,* given just what she'd been through already. How much she'd been made to endure.

Teeth bared, she redoubled her efforts. Carving the tapered tip of Hadim's cock, because she didn't need him or his knot—she was going to carve a dick from maple and see herself through this heat.

The dregs of the nest she'd made in her sleep mocked her. Nature laughing at her frail attempts to stop the inevitable, for no matter that she'd destroyed the fluffy snuggle-pit as many times as she's made it, she was driven by instinct now. One usually managed by the suppressors. At first, gathering the softest detritus she could find was little more than an irritating distraction. But in less than a day it had grown into an all-consuming need. One that stole sleep, bypassed hunger, and infected every infernal thought that floated through her sex-addled brains.

She *had* to build a nest.

How else would her young be safe and warm?

She hissed, clawing at her nape. Using the lancing pain to distract from that insane train of thought, only to find her skin raw and already bleeding. Self-inflicted wounds, forgotten over and over again.

There was no distraction capable of denying the fact that she'd already built *dozens* of nests. Improvised in the absence of luxurious furs, she'd built them obsessively, only to come to her senses and stomp her efforts into nothing. Kicking the discarded bits and pieces when her mind cleared of hated instinct. Instinct that hissed and raged, for no matter how perfect the construction, each and every one had been incomplete. Missing a fundamental piece she couldn't forage or create.

Missing Hadim—or more specifically, his salty, sticky come.

Disgusted, she abandoned her carving project, tossing the wooden cock aside. A wasted effort that couldn't work, not without a cunt full of sperm and a knot to seal it inside. Her spear shortened for nothing.

She swallowed, throat clicking. Treacherous quim growing plump and needy with little more than the thought of being mounted by the male she hated more with every breath. Every instant of separation from the life she'd abandoned.

But if Hadim were here now... she knew she'd beg. With one breath of his scent, she'd scream for more as he pressed her into her shitty nest. Plead him to fuck her until her womb was seeded. Cry until her voice was raw.

Her chest grew tight. Sopping wet where she ached to be stretched, she fought for every breath to come easy, yet knew it was almost upon her. Knew the heat would addle what was left of her faculties... that it was going to be worse than anything she'd ever experienced thus far.

If she belonged to a harem, the matrons would have guided her through a natural season. They would have prepared her in the old ways—with oils, soft hands, and calming song once the breeding was through. They'd braid her hair and nurse any mating wounds she'd earned, blue eyes shimmering with understanding and cutting humor, but not pity. Never that.

But she *didn't* belong to a harem, and blue eyes would never shimmer again.

Out here she was alone. Beyond the crust of civilization, criminals roamed. Dangerous males who hadn't caught a female's scent since they'd been tossed over the wall—if ever. Their tails docked to mark them as other, they were unfit to belong. Criminals. Rejects and outcasts maimed for the things they'd done.

Like her.

By the fires, if one of them caught wind of her pheromones?

She'd *wish* for the days of being a mere concubine.

There'd be no detached, efficient breeding and months' worth of solitude. No harem full of Hathorian females to share the burden and no soothing hands or watchful matrons.

She'd be lucky if she weren't fucked to death by a horde of desperate Anhur males.

No, she was trapped out here on the edge, her scent screaming of fertility, thighs tacky with slick. But was she doomed to submit to the first males lucky enough to stumble across her? Or... or could she make something of herself that was more than a sex slave and breeder?

Something that could thrive in the wilds... something like Samina...

Glimmering overhead, the moons peaked between the clouds. A gust of heated summer wind held whispered hints of what she needed, thick with the scent she craved. What it would take to end her torment.

Males.

Distant, yet. But there all the same.

Her pelvic muscles screamed and ached, begging to be stretched beyond all reasonable limits.

Once her heat settled in, all else would be pushed out. All but the need for teeth and seed. Pummeling hips.

Hadim's knot.

Taking a breath, she threw back her head

and howled at the three moons hanging ever-present and low on the horizon. Fury bristling, silky black hair whipped about her face as she screamed her angst into the evening chill. Howled until her voice splintered and broke, until her breath came on a gasp and some of the fervor abated.

If she wanted to retain some semblance of sanity, she'd *have* to find a male. She'd have to sort through these rejects and monsters and find one capable of seeing her through a brutal heat. One that she could discard just as easily, while she searched the wilds for enough yarrow root to keep her womb in pristine condition.

Decision made, she gathered her supplies, and with only a moment's hesitation, retrieved her shoddy wooden cock.

Just in case.

F lushed with renewed purpose, she turned her nose into the breeze. Searching for the hint of wet vegetation that would indicate a water source, for if there were males to be found, it would be by the water.

She didn't have to search long.

It was a modest creek. One without a great deal of volume, perhaps, but sweet enough to drink even if it carried a hint of sulfur.

She dipped her hands then pressed them to her nape, trying to cool herself. And it was then, as she knelt by the edge staring at her reflection, that she recalled faded blue eyes. That to soak in cool water was to soothe the ache of a heat denied.

Fully clothed, she waded into the stream. Sucking in a deep, calming breath, for this was usually a risk she didn't take. Washing away the stench of the dead was a foolish luxury she could ill afford.

Survival this long in the wilds beyond the crust depended on her ability to suffer. To endure without adequate hygiene, knowing she would never be able to build a shelter by a ready supply of water, for if there was ease to be had out here in the beyond? It was a locale worth fighting over. Drawing in desperate males from every caste.

And draw them in, she would.

A hint of warmth twisted around her fingers. Even through her sodden leathers, she felt it kiss the flesh of her thighs and knew she'd found the place to set her trap.

Hot water that stank of sulfur? In the beyond, that meant only one thing—this stream was fed by a thermal vent.

Grinning now, she trudged through the water. Splashing and careless, she followed the creek north until she came to a fork. The main current split right, but the left climbed toward a clearing in the dense forest, and it was *hot*.

She scrambled over the bank and found the clearing to be flat red stone with no ground cover. What must have been an ancient riverbed, it had been worn but wasn't smooth, and she could see where eddies had carved swirling circles into the surface. Where the layers of sediment that had settled over thousands of years had solidified. And, boots slapping against the wet, red stone, she jogged toward the source of hot water. Eyes flicking around the barren landscape ringed by trees.

A series of three hot springs, each on their own stone ledge. The uppermost pool drained into the bottom two, connecting them all to the main creek below. Careful, feeling her heat return as her temperature rose, she picked her way to the top. Dipping her fingers in each pool as she passed, she found them warm and deep. It all came from the largest pool, where a small underground stream met the surface. A heated stream that had once been vigorous enough to carve a cave from solid granite.

Hesitating, ears pricked and straining for any hint that the cave might be occupied, she froze at the entrance. Hearing not so much as a hint of life, she picked up a rock and tossed it into the dark. Ready to flee.

But when nothing came roaring into the light, she grinned. Absently rubbing at her cleft through the leather.

It was perfect, really. A secluded niche where she could rut with her chosen males until they were spent and drained. Far enough away from their camp to afford her a little privacy, she could trap them on *her* terms.

The ache pulsed through her system, eager for a male to pound it into submission.

Mouth watering, she turned to look over the clearing. At the forest line, and from this distance, she could see the shadow of three main game trails. All easy to traverse through the dense foliage—even easier to sprint straight into a trap.

Yet although a plan was beginning to form, anxious sweat dampened her brow.

If she failed... this was it. Her last day of freedom and she'd spend it enslaved to her most basic instinct.

Something akin to fear skated down her back but tugged at her sex. Making it clench and gush, because it was already too late to do anything else.

What was fear to a Hathorian but another sort of lubricant?

There was nothing gentle about enduring a true rut, always an element of uncertain terror with an Anhur master like Hadim. She'd been conditioned to be wet and ready at the first hint of danger—but there was every possibility that she'd draw in the wrong sort of attention. That she'd find herself enslaved to an Anhur with the potential to be much, *much* worse than Hadim had ever been. Though her master had been cruel, it was a flavor she'd known well. A brand she'd grown accustomed to, no matter the sour aftertaste.

There wasn't time to be clever, not now, with her *Biquea* glands ripe enough to burst.

Swollen and aching, it wouldn't be long before she couldn't help herself. Before she resorted to fucking any bottom-dweller or reject lucky enough to stumble across her in such a state. If he had a prick or tongue or protuberance of literally any kind, she'd fling herself at, on, or over it and beg for more.

She'd seen it happen in the Harem. To the females who'd matured faster than she, who succumbed to their first breeding with sweet laughs and eager smiles. Hated watching her friends become *less than* as their eyes glazed over and their tails lifted in invitation. Their ears standing rigid in eager anticipation.

And then Hadim would ruin them, taking pride in their downcast eyes. The way their tails tucked whenever he was near, their ears drooping terrified in submission.

Not for her.

Not anymore, for she had no tail to tuck. Nothing to broadcast her fear, except her scent itself—and *that* she'd buried beneath a fresh layer of dead man's fat, harvested from the first corpse she'd come across.

No, this time they'd come to *her*. This time she'd choose her suitor and ignore those who weren't worthy of tainting her bloodlines.

Teeth flashing, she got to work.

Built fail-safes, twisting rope and setting traps until her fingers bled. Cursing under her breath with such vehemence that spittle sprayed between clenched teeth, she worked until her attention began to splinter. Until her every waking thought was not about maintaining her freedom, but dulling the ache throbbing between her thighs with something thick and warm and spurting.

But when her preparations were finally made, it was with time enough to watch the first moon rise. A full moon, it was the first of the three sisters to ripen, bathing the clearing in a soft white glow.

It was time to set the bait.

Stripping out of her leathers, she went nude to the forest's edge. Long cloak slung over her shoulders.

And then, swiping her left hand through the slick dripping between glistening thighs, she rubbed it across the trunk of a tree. Her every sense primed for a hint that she'd been discovered, she rushed to mark a trail through the underbrush. The chore giving her much needed distraction as she fought to ignore the ache scratching at the back of her pelvis.

She painted erratic tracks all the way back

to the stream, fingers leaving sticky trails of slick wherever her touch landed. Leaving droplets of slick in her wake, she grew bolder with every passing second.

And then she heard voices.

9

Diving into the shadows behind a tree, she slipped into her cloak. Fingers dancing over the buttons, the scent of putrefying corpse engulfing her once again.

She'd found a camp.

One simple, shoddy tent erected in a clearing around a rocky outcropping. A fire pit complete with roasting meat. The smell hanging ripe and alluring in a forest filled with ravenous predators who wouldn't fear the light of a fire.

Her stomach twisted, rejecting the mere idea of food this close to her season. But beneath it, a scent she'd been craving.

Males.

Arrogant enough not to care, or too new to the wood to understand the peril, they lived boldly. Out in the open.

Driven by instinct, she oozed through the underbrush, reeking of death. Belly down, her hood pulled low over her eyes, she blended into the detritus. Pressing forward until she was close enough to hear the low rumble of conversation.

"You want half?"

She blinked, peering through the gloom to identify the speaker.

Two large Anhur males sat side by side, tending a cooking fire. Sharing something roasted on a spit, the one on the left set his teeth to a hank of meat as the other chewed. Mechanical. Precise. The muscle in his jaw bulging with every clench of his teeth. His profile defined and rugged. Jaw sharp, if rough with stubble. His face too washed out by the firelight to determine eye color as anything beyond 'pale'.

"We're running low on meat," he said, and she scowled. Pulling her eyes away from the subtle hints of masculinity. Annoyed that it took so little to make her gush and squirm, that she was aroused by watching them eat.

"I'll send Keever and Micah out tomorrow," said the other, this one almost as large as Hadim himself, his back to her. The Alpha of this small pack, presumably—she recognized the edge of authority when it rumbled through his vocal cords. "And Sickle?"

"Still in bed," came the gruff reply. "Sulking, far as I can tell."

The Alpha snorted and tossed his scraps into the fire—she saw the sparks leap. "Vain little thing, isn't he?"

"Pathetic," the second sneered, hackles bristling in profile. "Even the hybrids are bitching about it, as if none of us know what it is to be docked."

This was a pack of unmated Anhur and hybrid males, then. Apparently new to life in the beyond.

Her stump gave a sympathetic twinge in remembrance, the phantom of that beloved fifth limb tucking between her thighs as if she could protect it after all this time.

"I'll have a chat with him," the Alpha said, and stood, his face obscured from where she skulked. He clapped his hands against his backside. A backside that was thick with muscle she couldn't help but watch until it disappeared into the camp's only tent. And even though the absence of his tail made her heart sink, she knew it would be held high. In the manner of all dominant Anhur, no matter their gender.

She needed to leave. One Anhur was an insane risk—but two, *plus* a handful of hybrid males?

They'd force her submission in an instant, all her planning would go to rot.

No, what she needed was a lone hybrid. A *sterile* hybrid male who was bigger than an Anhur.

Even if they didn't have the most potent sperm or... or the biggest knot. A Beta was safe.

She swallowed, clenching her thighs together, spine tingling with the threat of an unprovoked orgasm. One she fought, for to get caught now, without a plan, was to become a slave to these unknown males.

When next she could focus her attention on the camp, the Alpha had already returned and reclaimed his seat. His back to her once more—at his side, a slender *Hathorian* male.

Sucking in a breath, she lurched forward. Ears pressed flat to her skull, hood slipping back to reveal her face, the stench of fear began to seep through her camouflage.

An elegant little blond, all slim lines and soft edges. His ears left intact, the graceful shells flickering back and forth. Tipped in a golden sheen, the hair within was kept trim and soft. Groomed.

But if the mussed hair, smudged kohl, and bleary gaze was any indication, he didn't appear to be adapting to life in the beyond very well.

Or he was being abused by this pack.

Tortured... *raped.*

Hathorian males were almost as rarely seen as the females.

They were pets. Traded amongst Anhur queens and trained to please in all ways. Aesthetic perfection, they bore the whims of their mistresses. Decorated in piercings and swirling tattoos, each trendier than the last.

This delicate creature was the first she'd ever seen.

"I'm not hungry," he said, a lilting symphony of soft tones edged with an alluring hint of something gruff. Or perhaps his voice was merely strained, as if he'd invested a lot of time in noisy weeping.

"Eat it anyway," the Alpha said and passed him the last portion of roasted meat, his voice heavy with a wisp of familiarity that made her shudder.

The command, perhaps. Or the tone. Whatever it was, it made the born submissive inside her shiver and present. Losing focus long enough to make her spine flex where she would have lifted her tail in desperate, sordid invitation.

Oblivious to the female in need, the Alpha continued to press his command. Unyielding, until the dainty male huffed, accepting with a graceless pout. "We're packing up in the morning, Sickle," the Alpha continued, voice laden with gentle reprimand. "You need to keep your strength up."

Shoulders slumping, Sickle nodded. Utterly defeated even as he began to chew, taking tiny bites. But though Sickle's posture was meek, he didn't flinch when the Alpha clapped his shoulder—he offered a weak smile that still managed to make her heart flutter with giddy excitement.

But the wonder of seeing her first Hathorian male paled in comparison to the absurdity of an Anhur miming kindness. How could Sickle stomach the Alpha's touch?

Baffled by such an outlandish notion, she

crept closer, trying to catch a glimpse of the Alpha's face so she could see what kind of monster she'd found in the wood. What brand of cruelty he offered Sickle in exchange for a smile like *that*?

The rest of the pack began to gather around the fire, not one among them seeming to roll over for this Alpha who ate and lounged with peasants.

"Who's on guard tonight?" the Alpha asked, his mane on full display where it traced the top third of his spine. Relaxed and at ease. Elbows on knees, leaning forward in a position the girl knew well—it allowed one to sit without bothering an amputation site.

"Keever and Konjo," the other Anhur replied, and took a long drink from a patchy water skin. His throat bobbing around each swallow.

But when the Alpha yawned and said, "Take Sickle with you. He's an asset," the other Anhur barked out a laugh.

"What's he going to do if they run across one of the infected, huh? Offer to make it pretty with a bit of fire ash?"

Sickle's demeanor grew sharp, his grin displaying pointed, intact teeth. It was a thing she'd only ever heard spoken of in reference to the procedure all female harem slaves went through. Filing the canines flat and blunt to protect their Anhur masters from damage during the rut.

To take away their only natural defense

and turn it into just another hole to be used. She ran her tongue over the smooth line of her teeth, her heart squelching painfully against her ribs.

It was the Alpha's turn to laugh, and he clapped Sickle's nape as he did so—then shifted into her line of sight.

The left side of his face shown in a shaft of flickering fire light.

Hadim.

He was here.

Right in front of her.

Come to collect his runaway slave.

And she was out of time, out of options, for with one glance she succumbed. Her body reacting to the memory of her master, of his knot as it filled and soothed. Spurting and kicking against that final gate, painting her cervix white with his thick, Anhur cream.

Muscles quivering in a fine shiver, she fought to remain still. Hidden. To deny the pull she felt to go to him. To take her punishment as she was meant and please the male who could make it all better...

Blunt teeth bared, her eyes snapped open. Ears twitched flat against her skull, hidden deep inside her cloak.

No.

She would suffer alone. Throw herself to the mercy of feral monsters and be torn apart, consumed alive before she ever allowed Hadim to touch her again.

No matter the danger, she retreated. Eyes

fixed to the pack, ears leveled out, she strained for any hint that she'd been discovered. Any hiccup in their low conversation that might warn her to pause, her breath held as terror pounded through her veins, for beneath her cloak of putrid rot, she was naked.

Vulnerable.

"We'll continue the hunt at first light," the Alpha said, then stood in one fluid motion. Turned and stepped over a fallen log. Moving toward her with sure, easy steps.

She froze.

Belly flat in the detritus, she dared only watch his approaching boots. Terrified to glance up, as if that would improve her chances of evasion.

He stopped at the forest's edge, uttered a clipped huff, and the whisper of laces through leather swished above her. A deep, masculine sigh and water splashed just beyond where she lay prone in the dirt.

Urine.

Male pheromones screaming of fertility and health. It'd been so long, she'd almost forgotten his scent. Almost didn't recognize her master.

A whimper squealed and died in her throat, scarcely loud enough to escape the leaf litter as Hadim relieved himself.

Her skin burned with aching, blistering need. Eyes falling shut, she squeezed them tight as they could go.

"Something reeks over here," he murmured, his voice rougher than she recalled. Unrecognizable, it was deeper. The new rasp vibrating straight through her nervous system, making her flex. Her slit oozing dangerously close to fresh air, where it might spill out and overpower the stench of her cloak.

She heard him shake, heard the last few drops as they were flung and spattered against the leaves.

But when he stepped back, giving a hop to adjust his pants, she dared a glance. Couldn't help the urge to see her master's face after all these months.

What she saw instead was enough to make her heart skip, lurching to an alarming halt before stuttering to life with an erratic flutter. A scream trapped in her throat.

Scars.

Four deep slashes raked down the right side of his face. Red and swollen, they'd healed *badly*, the tissue ridged and disfigured. His right eye cast in a milky, silver sheen. The pupil fixed in a narrow prick despite the darkening hour.

Mutilated by another Anhur. There was no mistaking the spread of those wicked claws, the damage that could be wrought with a single, vicious swipe. After all, she still bore the scars from the last time they'd met, her right arm ridged from armpit to wrist by Hadim's own touch.

A shiver rippled through her, skin crawling as she recalled another time she'd seen what Anhur claws might be capable of. Gooseflesh prickled the inside of her cloak where it clung and slid, soaked in anxious sweat. Her ears ringing with grotesque memory... *the sound of meat ripping from bone. The hiss of a dying breath where it spattered through a gaping hole made by Anhur claws...*

She tore her gaze away from his face, horrified. Banishing the specter with faded blue eyes behind several forceful blinks. Her breath leaking between dry lips, heart drumming inside her skull. Rushing in her ears.

And so she remained, cowering in the dirt, breath shallow enough to make her head spin, her lips tingle. Eyes squeezed shut until she heard the crunch of retreating boots.

The moment had passed. Hadim already back in his seat.

Desperate to escape, she continued her retreat.

Muscles trembling with exertion. Sweat soaking through her under-layer, making the greasy film of fat turn to liquid that threatened to drip into her eyes. Her open mouth.

And when she was far enough away, when she could run without the fear of discovery, she couldn't resist any longer.

Succumbing, she collapsed with one hand stuffed between her legs. Fingers squelching in the sodden mess she found there. Knowing that without a knot to squash her *Biquea* glands—milking them of the opiate that would soothe her burning nerves

—she'd be unable to do anything but make it worse. It was the unique anatomy of a knot, designed to keep her docile, tame, and sedated so she could be seeded with the next generation of warriors.

Groaning, she pulled out her carved cock, sinking to her knees in the dirt. Pleasure shivering through her muscles as the smooth wood slid between her lips.

Hadim's face—whole and without the horrific scars—flashed behind her lids. Teeth bared in a ravenous, mocking grin...

Gasping, she forced her eyes open. Staring at the canopy above.

Half-naked, stuffed with a wooden prick with no knot, she couldn't get there. The orgasm bubbling beneath her skin couldn't compete with her seething hatred for the master who'd made her a whore.

But...

What would it hurt? To go back without a plan, bend over, and demand to be mounted. To let him see her for the fierce, wild creature she'd become?

Shaking now, she fought to stand. Letting her cock slip free, it fell discarded in the leaf litter. Her cloak hanging from narrow shoulders, gaped wide and baring all. Fingers catching at a low branch, sticky and shining in the dim light, reeking of slick. Fertility.

"By the Nine," she whispered, sweating freely as lethargy washed over her. Hip pressed to the tree trunk, her gaze fixed on nothing as her chin tipped forward. Her level of awareness plummeting and distorted. "*No...*"

She had to get back. To her den... her nest. Before Hadim...

"Hadim's coming," she mumbled, pupils expanding in a dazed ring. One ear tipped forward, the other back. "Have to lure them." Tasting the air, she pushed her fingers through tangled hair. Head tipping to the side, her brow knit in confusion. "No..." A lazy shake of her head. "Laid a trail already..." She took a step—stumbled. Her ears flicking forward and back, twitching at every tiny sound. "Just have to wait..."

Thighs tacky as she stumbled along, she tripped over a fallen log. Her palms skinning before she caught herself. Panting. Disoriented.

Eyes glassy, her ears drooped. Jaw hanging slack as slick oozed between plump lips. Making her shudder as it dripped.

"Please..." she whispered, her voice splintering around a keening wail. Hands flying to the bones framing her mound, where it hurt and throbbed. "*Please...*"

She *needed* a knot. To be mounted and stretched.

But not... *that* knot.

Determination sharpened her gaze. A beacon of defiance shining bright in the fog, she trudged on. Following the river back to her den.

Hadim would *never* get the chance to see her grow round with his brats.

She wouldn't let him.

"Just have to... soak in the water," she said, shuddering. Every step sending a bolt of agonized pleasure zinging through her nerves. "Glands will be smaller"—a gasp hissed through her teeth—"heat will be better."

The smooth red stone came into view as she rounded a corner, the fog thick with a biting edge of sulfur. Thermal vent actively bubbling where it hissed and spit, lending a tempting twist of warmth to the evening breeze.

"Heat..." Luminous eyes turned into the warm wind. "Heat makes it better," she said, heading *not* to the cooling creek, but to the hot springs.

Confused, *helpless*, she dropped into the uppermost hot spring with a low hiss as the heat seeped deep into her muscles.

Core temperature spiking, and with it, her arousal.

Slick gushed between her legs, mixing with each swirl of heated water. Filling the pool with the potent pheromones unique to her pedigree... before it was carried downstream.

10

Clenching his fist just to feel his claws extend, the Alpha stared into the flames.

Blind in his right eye. Depth perception ruined, the wounds still festered all these many moons later. And yet, it always took a moment to adjust to the black wall that was his new blind spot.

"It's looking better," Sickle said, dabbing at the corner of the Alpha's ruined eye with a warm compress. Tending old wounds with a delicate touch—a welcome relief to the heated, ever-present itch of lingering infection.

A parting gift from his father.

"I think using the scarab beetles improved the scar tissue," Sickle said, squinting, a frown creasing the Hathorian's tattooed brow as he manipulated the tight, thick skin. "Does it still itch?"

The Alpha took a breath, but was cut off by the approach of his second.

"Quit fussing," Balkazar snapped, mane flaring briefly in warning before he settled on the Alpha's good side. "Doesn't need your motherin', boy. *He'll live.*"

Startled, Sickle stepped back as if struck. Arms crossed around his ribs, massive velvety ears pressed flat against fluffy blond hair. "Scars can cause horrible pain if they're left untreated—especially on the face."

"Scars've been there for what, six months now?" the war chief chuckled, claws extended as he scratched at his jaw. Eyes locked on the slender male's decorated face—the gaze of a predator looking for a fight. "Leave it alone," Balkazar rasped. "They're healed."

Soft Hathorian features grew hard, and Sickle took a breath. Determination settling into his every muscle, he flashed sharp teeth at the war chief, then dipped his fingers in a warming pot beside the fire. Brandishing a fresh cloth soaked in the stinging scent of medicinal herbs. "All I'm doing is—"

"*Fretting,*" Balkazar drawled, goading the slender male. Legs crossed at the ankles, lips twisted in a derisive sneer. "You're motherin'. And unless you're aiming to lift the tail for him and sate his rut, piss off."

"*Fine.*" Color touched the Hathorian's decorated cheeks, a band of heat glowing pink across the bridge of his nose. "If you have need of me, I'll be *motherin'* the new recruits. And that's a willow bark and peppermint compress," he added, meeting the Alpha's one-eyed gaze. "It'll help with the swelling and itching. Leave it on until the cloth goes cold, unless you'd prefer to suffer."

The Anhur males were silent as they watched him go, but it was the war chief whose lips parted over a grin. "Good for him. Nice to see the boy finding his balls, eh? Didn't even call you Alpha once."

"He's older than you are," the Alpha said, his claws extending once more. Straining not to scratch.

Balkazar shrugged. "Then it's about time he grew a spine." Jerking his chin in the direction Sickle had gone, toward the trio of hybrids working to take down their tent, the war chief said, "Just need a few more recruits like those three, and we'll be on our way."

The Alpha snorted, not bothering himself to engage with this argument again. To do as Balkazar demanded and build an army of rejects in the beyond. Storm the Silver City. Take vengeance for being exiled and stripped of his inheritance. His army of hybrids had been slaughtered, his harem seized, pillaged of hard-won noble Hathorian bloodlines that had produced fine, powerful hybrids.

All of his females had no doubt been distributed amongst the Sultan's favored sons. Any hybrids still on the breast dead or made into eunuchs.

He had nothing.

No longer was he a favored son of the Karahmet bloodline, but an exile. No better than any other he might rule.

To fight back now was hopeful nonsense —he'd been dealt a mortal blow. Knew when to yield, where the war chief did not.

As execution of a Firstborn son was forbidden, he'd been sentenced to a lifetime of wandering in the wilds. Cast out as custom demanded, he'd been given nothing but the life of his war chief and was made to watch the others fall beneath the blade.

His father had laughed as their sentence was dealt. Cooing in mock remorse as his favored son was banished, docked, hybrid sons slaughtered, his harem ravished. No longer a threat to his father's vast holdings. His title. And then his father had taken his mother's favorite pet behind his golden, Hathorian ears, and shoved him into unwilling arms. "A parting gift to see you through the withdrawal."

As if a prince would sully himself with a queen's plaything!

No, he'd gone through the withdrawal alone. Without his Omegas, without a harem of dedicated females to induce his rut and catch his seed. The testosterone burning as it was purged from his system, and *still*, not an instant of unwanted attention was paid to his father's final gift. Sickle left unmolested, if traumatized by the abrupt change in living circumstances.

From pampered pet to survivor.

But through it all, the war chief held out hope. Even after all these long months of the hunt, after only managing to find *three* hybrids that weren't infected with the Trax virus, Balkazar continued his hunt. With one lone male and two underfed brothers to show for it.

Hardly an army of blood-thirsty rebels, though Konjo and Keever certainly had the appetites of several dozen males.

At the rate they were going, generations of the royal blood would rise and fall before his ragged pack could gather the resources to attack.

If they survived the winter—and all the beasts who would awaken with the first snow. Those who hibernated while the summer children were fattened by long months of easy meals.

The Alpha hadn't the luxury of hope. Knew just what lurked in the wilds, for he'd seen it when he was a child. His father had taken he and his siblings into the beyond to impress a young Anhur consort. Guarded by a hundred of his hybrid sons, he'd sent his natural children out of the carriage so he might breed a female that was not their mother.

And then the wilds attacked.

A wave of ravenous predators descended

from the skies. Raining acid and cooing over blistering wounds, they'd formed a beautiful, deadly cloud. Tiny winged lizards who sang while they feasted. The swarm capable of bringing down blooded warriors by the dozens, he'd watched his only sister crushed to death beneath the weight of her personal guard.

It was only the beginning of the horrors that came pouring from the wood while the carriage rocked above them. His father serenading his new treasure to the sounds of death and horror.

Nearly seventy hybrids died that day—and every one of his siblings.

But he survived. He alone was showered in praise, named Firstborn, and given every advantage afforded him by his position of favor.

No matter how many new siblings his father gave him—of which there were many dozens—he was the one who stood at his father's side. Groomed to one day challenge the Sultan himself.

No more. Not after—

"Alpha!"

His hackles bristled, mood soured by the hated shades of the past, by the sound of a hybrid's voice that was not one of his own.

"My Alpha, *please!* You must come!"

Turning left, into his line of sight, the Alpha glared at the hybrid jogging across their camp. One of the twins. Konjo. An unmistakable silhouette clenched in his large hand.

Smooth. Polished. It was a carved length of maple, complete with veins and bulbous glans.

"Is that—" the Alpha swallowed, his attention caught by the breath of the sweet impossible scent wafting from between the hybrid's thick fingers. The words died on his tongue.

His brain stuttered to a grinding halt, recognizing that scent in an instant.

And for a long moment, as he stared at the thing being presented to him, he couldn't speak. Couldn't do much of anything really, except gape at what was clenched in Konjo's fist. Stupefied.

And then, "Is that a cock?"

"Yes, my Alpha," Konjo replied, his voice a deep gravelly rumble, his eyes unable to break away from the false phallus. Pupils narrowed to tiny points of black. "It stinks of"— the hybrid swallowed, then glanced over his shoulder as he whispered, "*slick*. It even tastes of slick... but..." He licked his lips. "But it can't be, right?"

Heart pounding against his ribs, the Alpha snatched the shaft with careful fingers. Inspecting the carving with a critical eye, he breathed deep of a scent he thought he'd never know again. Committing it to memory, he grew familiar with her on an intimate level. Knew the scent of her... the taste...

Mouth watering, his tongue darted out to lick the wooden dildo from base to tip.

At the first hint of that precious flavor, his sack tightened. The rut threatening to consume him in a rush—mind growing hazy with ecstasy. His cock surging against his inseam.

It was enough. Enough to know that she was near, in the wild, her quim dripping and swollen. Needy.

A young Hathorian female, escaped from her cage. Running free in the beyond.

And the little runaway was recklessly close to a natural season, her slick already flowing. Ripe and potent. A rival to the very best of *any* female his harem had once boasted, the Alpha knew the sheen of quality for what it was.

Her bloodline was ancient and robust. The bouquet of her slick crisp, the flavor buttery, hers was a treasured lineage—one he recognized by scent alone. A gem worthy of the Sultan's private stock, she was a female equal to whelping the next generation trained to die in defense of their sire. Her traits hand-chosen to protect royal blood, she'd been bred from noble, beloved Omegas horded by the elite.

By him, once.

In the Silver City, she would have been a treasure.

But out here, in the wild beyond? She was the breath of the Nine, a cleansing wave of molten earth. A beacon of hope where diseased males roamed, her womb slavering for a knot to stuff her full of Anhur seed.

The Alpha smiled, his scars doing nothing to soften the edge stark need that spread across his features.

"What's all this?"

Startled, the Alpha whirled, a snarl erupting from curled lips. Reeking of the rut, his hormones spiked as the war chief drew near. Balkazar. The only other male capable of fighting to claim this mysterious female. Of taking what was *his* by birthright.

A male with perfect depth perception, but who'd never run a harem before. Loyal and beyond reproach. A deadly Anhur male in the prime of his life, who didn't know rut like *he* knew rut.

Even now, he felt it. The familiar rush as it began—a drug he'd long been addicted to, as all Anhur with large harems were addicted. Trying for subtlety and failing, he adjusted his swollen, dribbling prick. Sack drawn tight, dumping testosterone directly into his bloodstream. And so he would remain, teetering on the edge of violence until he'd hunted her down, filled her to overflowing, and ridden her through her season.

Only when that slight female belly began to swell with a litter of his kits, would he relent. His work done, until her scent grew thick and ripe once more.

Hackles rising in spite of himself, the

Alpha took a breath and forced, "We've got ourselves a runaway," through bared and clenched teeth.

Excitement gleamed in the war chief's eyes. "Caught the scent of another hunt? Anhur this time?"

"Better," the Alpha said, and pressed the wooden cock into Balkazar's hands. Fighting to uncurl clenched fingers.

The war chief's eyes went wide, his nostrils pinched white. "Lord and Lady All-Gods, *what*—that smell—"

"Slick," the Alpha said. Hackles raised and bushy, the back of his neck and shoulders tight.

"Breeder," Balkazar returned, pupils shrinking as the rut threatened to consume him, too. Her scent a powerful lure. "And a crafty little bitch to make such a thing!" The war chief grunted, knuckles going white as he took in the faceless female's scent. "But how is that possible? How could she be here at all?"

The Alpha shrugged. "A runaway from the foundling colony. Or perhaps a wealthy lord took one of his bitches into the wood to rut like the ancients, and the wilds fought back," he said, teeth gleaming white in the firelight. Grin growing feral, his cock throbbed at the thought. Of taking her in the old ways, triggering her cycle without the aid of oils and herbs. "It doesn't matter," he rasped. "She'll be mine soon."

But it was Balkazar's turn to smile, the

gesture making the Alpha's nape tighten in wary preparedness. "No, brother," the war chief said, passing a cautious thumb over the tip of the wooden phallus. "She'll be *ours*. From her womb, an army will march on the Silver City."

11

Taking a deep breath, Balkazar turned his mind to the task, pleased. A hunt.

A proper hunt for the most valuable treasure in the beyond.

And what a hunt it was turning out to be!

Not only had the saucy little minx left them a wild trail to follow, *she'd done it in slick.* The forethought alone was enough to boggle the mind, for he'd seen enough of the vacant glassy eyes to know—Omegas in heat were gluttons for but one thing. Denying food, water, and sleep until they'd gotten stuffed and sealed.

Mindless drones who'd do anything for a knot.

On the cusp of a natural season, this female had the nerve to taunt when she should have been begging.

Balkazar grinned, rolling his neck until it popped.

This was what he did best. Hunt. Before he'd been recruited, his skill had made him infamous in the black markets. Specialized in trafficking drugs, goods, and of course, females.

It was what had brought he and the prince together, all those years ago. He, born without standing, a smuggler of precious goods, supplying breeding females to the Firstborn Son of the Karahmet bloodline.

He'd expected the prince to be yet another of the fat and lazy Alphas lounging in the safety of a palatial home. Those who promised a better life, access to females, to a future that didn't end young and bloody. Enslaved to the perfume of hope, Balkazar and his pack had kept those insatiable gluttons supplied with a steady diet of high-quality pussy and illicit goods. Ensured their ranks continued to swell with hybrids whelped from stolen breeders.

Every single one of the upper class guilty of the exact same crimes. Who punished the common folk for daring to exist in the system *they'd* created.

But the prince was different. He saw the hypocrisy for what it was, knew all the grimy details commoners could only guess to be true.

Not a one of the most beloved conspiracy theories came *close* to the horrible truth. None might guess how deep the rot had crept into the Silver City.

The laws designed to protect them all, little more than wisps of fragile lies that hardly bothered to be convincing. All but undone by the wants of a ruling class that had armies of hybrids to die for them. Who squashed rebellions before they became more than whispers, no matter that one male claiming dozens of females had unbalanced the gender ratios and created instability for the young males *not* in a position to simply take what they wanted. That in doing so, roving packs of unattached males were forced to hunt together. Kill together. And though it wasn't spoken of, some were even known to fuck each other to relieve the misery of being utterly without options.

These were the problems of peasants. Of those too weak to compete for resources.

So males like Balkazar did what they had to do. They adapted to the misery of the way things were, or they died before their undesirable genes could be passed down.

Simple.

Unavoidable.

Brutal.

Until the Firstborn had let Balkazar sire a few kits of his own on an Omega bitch in the harem.

They'd bred her together.

One driving the other deeper into rut. The presence of another male—the scent of royal seed mixed with high-quality slick—had sparked a heated rush of hormones that only made Balkazar's rut sweeter. To have slick on tap, any time he wanted it? The prince eager to rut at his side?

It was a luxury he'd only ever dared to dream of.

The moons rose and fell three times before their breeder whelped her litter. And though most bore the vibrant green eyes of their sire, there were two who gazed at him with eyes he'd seen every day in the mirror.

A gift he would not soon forget, one that bought loyalty the war chief would never question.

That the prince had been made to go without... the throbbing, twisting agony of withdrawal from slick and the rut it inspired? It was his fault. *He* was the reason the prince had lost everything. Challenged his father too soon and been maimed for the oversight. One green eye lost its vibrant depth, the Alpha's face mutilated by a vicious swipe of his father's claws.

But it could have been *much* worse.

If he'd been any but a son of Karahmet, he'd have been executed immediately. The prince had demanded exile, his right as the named Firstborn—and of all the advisers and noble elite who'd stood with him, the prince had chosen Balkazar to join him. Knowing what it meant for the others.

That to do so meant sacrificing a limb and giving up any notion of standing within the walls of the Silver City ever again.

But Balkazar had never bothered to blame the disgraced prince for his docked tail. Instead, he'd turned that bitter resentment back to those who'd earned it. Those who hid behind policies they wrote and knew just how to break the rules without consequence.

He was a war chief. Elevated through the ranks to stand at the ear of his prince, Balkazar would endure the absence of rut. The withdrawal that never really left his system. A living torture where every passing day without a female made temptation of Sickle's sleek lines and willowy, Hathorian muscle. The memory of rut an insidious worm burrowing through brain matter. Boring holes and tunnels that all led back to slick heat and the flow of sticky fluids.

Balkazar couldn't image what it was for the prince, who'd been breeding his harem since his balls had dropped.

But now they had something to live for! A chance to make something of their pitiful lives in the beyond.

By the fires, it was their turn to breed an unwilling female. And with her, they would have an army.

He would train new generations to hate the Silver City as they ought. To carry out the designs of their sire as he bred more to die against the wall...

Balkazar would see his Alpha on the Sultan's throne, a female perched atop his cock, scepter dangling loose from clawed fingers, his thighs wet with slick. And perhaps, if the prince allowed it, a few hybrids would look up at Balkazar with familiar eyes and know of their sire's deeds. That his sperm had swum beside royalty and *won*.

Tipping his head back, Balkazar took a great, huffing inhale of the warm evening breeze. Eyes fluttering closed, hair tossed about his face. She was there on the wind. Hidden. And now that he had the scent of her, Balkazar could tell she'd been close to their camp. Clever enough to observe before she made her presence known, to disguise her scent beneath the putrid stench of death.

But there was a teasing hint of her pheromones still lingering in the places she'd most recently been. Hard to distinguish from the overwhelming scent of slick hanging heavy all around him, but he knew from ex-perience just how easy it would be to track her once their hunt was under way.

Now that he had her scent, the cloak of rot and death she'd wrapped around herself wouldn't matter.

It never did.

Even for clever ones who needed to be broken in.

Females rarely slowed to disguise their tracks—they ran. Tiny, female brains des-perate for the chase, they'd succumb to in-stinct. To find them already sopping wet was a perk of the job he'd loved best.

It was a biological dance long played between their species. A game of hunt and chase Balkazar never grew tired of playing.

"Ready the hybrids," he said, gruff. Adjusting the bulge pressing at the back of his inseam.

"I—I'm coming too," Sickle said, his eyes bright. Ears flicked forward. "I've never seen a Hathorian female before."

For a moment, as Balkazar regarded the slender, decorated male, he considered his response from the side of his eye. Arms crossed over burly chest, legs firmly planted at shoulder width. Not one to be swayed by emotion, it was his impulse to forbid such a reckless and needless demand. To protect the valuable, insufferable little thing and force him to submit as an Omega ought.

But the war chief did not intend to earn the loyalty of his brothers by being impulsive and cruel. So, with a sigh, he shook the tension from his nape and offered a tense nod, returning his gaze to the forest's edge. "Keep back and stay low. You're useless in a fight."

Blushing, Sickle's gaze found the earth. "Okay."

Balkazar and the Alpha had hoarded the dildo between them, any meager hint of slick had been lapped up before any of the pack might ask for a taste. Slick was for the *Anhur*, a precious libation that induced rut.

Still, Balkazar couldn't help noticing the ginger, mincing steps or the scent of arousal that hung heavy in Sickle's wake. Her scent potent enough to enthrall each and every member of their pack without so much as uttering a spoken word.

This would not be an easy hunt for any of them. Slick compelled a male to mate, left them all in a state of constant agonized arousal until they could find a female to relieve the tension.

What she'd done was cruel—*not* the behavior of a born submissive, but something else.

A queen.

The thought made the war chief drip. Sticky and hot against his leathers.

First, they were going to run her down. Toy with her fear, the way she'd toyed with them. Dragging it out as only experienced hunters could. And then, when she couldn't take another step, when she trembled with fatigue and her eyes shone with helpless lust, they'd take everything else.

Break her down and remake her as their obedient little slave. Come-drunk and mewling for more. Even when she was laden with young, they'd continue breeding her. Until she knew her place at their feet and 'escape' had been deleted from her lexicon.

It was the Anhur who'd get her first. Rutting until their lusts were satisfied, their balls drained and knots deflated.

Only then would they allow the hybrids a chance.

Poor Sickle would take what remained of their Hathorian female who'd claimed too much.

The Alpha—no longer a prince—appeared at Balkazar's side. Blinded, disfigured, but still every bit the cunning noble he'd come to think of as a brother, still the Alpha he'd follow into the wilds without a moment's hesitation.

"Ready?" Balkazar asked, his voice gruff with eager restraint.

Ceding the hunt to his war chief, the Alpha nodded, for no matter how skilled a leader he might have been, Balkazar was their hunter. The one with the sharpest instincts. Absent the fancy technology employed by those lazy twats hiding behind their precious wall, his skills were the best they had.

It was *all* they had, really.

And until he could train more, they'd need it—trying to follow the fragmented mind of a female losing her senses to a natural season wasn't easy. Bore no resemblance to logic in any form. Already they'd been trying to unravel her trail for hours, but the reward for success was too great to ignore.

Adjusting himself, the war chief watched Sickle stoop at the water's edge and drink from the stream.

"Fire-kin turn me to ash," Sickle groaned, then plunged his head beneath the surface. Drinking great gulps of sweet water without coming up for air. Didn't surface, in fact, until Balkazar himself pulled him up.

Sickle gasped, still swallowing. And then, "There's slick in the water." He lunged, trying again for the quietly bubbling stream. Fool enough to drown himself for another taste of that which was rare in the beyond.

"Stop!" Balkazar snarled, shaking Sickle by the lapels of his fitted leather jacket. "Think, boy. If her slick is in the water, what does that mean? Where will we find our bitch in heat?"

For several long moments, Sickle could do nothing but blink, straining toward the dilute slick. And then, "The water. She's upstream."

"To work, then," Balkazar grumbled, grinning.

Oh, he was going to enjoy this...

12

Sprinting as fast as his legs could go, Sickle ran with his brothers. Their feet falling sure and even, thighs whispering over well-worn leathers. Anhur before and behind, hybrids covering his flanks.

It was the safest he'd felt since he'd been taken by the scruff and tossed out. Unprovoked.

The new recruits to their sorry pack of six were hybrids. Big, as the mongrels often were, and bred for war. To defend their Alpha and his interests. Thundering along at his side, yet not daring to outpace him, they protected the weakest member by running at his speed.

It had always been this way for Sickle. The knowledge that he was less—smaller, slower, and not nearly as strong as even the female Anhur—had been the only real constant in his life.

Traded amongst the queens, he'd served

several dozen mistresses before his twentieth birthday. Only three had bothered to learn his name before growing bored of his talents.

And even *they'd* traded him for another without a hint of regret.

Trained and conditioned from birth to relish the honor of service, their lives were elegance and heartbreak. Joyous and cruel. All any Hathorian male would ever know was to kneel for an Anhur queen. To sing and to please, to be submissive when his queen needed an outlet.

Except for him.

Sickle's last queen hadn't uttered a word of protest as he was cast out on a cruel whim. Not one word. She'd laughed along with the rest as her husband made a mockery of his entire species.

"Here." The mistress's husband took Sickle by the nape, two claws curving around and hooking into the sensitive shell of his left ear. "A parting gift to see you through the withdrawal."

For weeks after they'd been cast out, Sickle had looked to the Firstborn with glassy-eyed terror. Certain the son would heed the father's advice and vent the dregs of a lasting rut in his body. It was known to happen, after all. To those foolish enough to defy their mistress, who stole, or dared to strike at the clawed fist that held their leash.

Those unfortunates were discarded, left to die in the streets. Abandoned in the farthest slums, they were snatched up by packs of roving, unattached males. Desperate for a soft touch...

But Sickle had been banished beyond the wall no matter how prettily he begged.

Grinding his teeth, he redoubled his effort, nipping at the war chief's heels.

No, he'd been cast out. Exiled. But there were mercies. Balkazar had a hurtfully low opinion of his kind—especially females. But he'd fought just as hard as the Alpha to win Sickle's trust. Instead of taking liberties, they'd given him weapons. Taught him to shoot, to hunt, and to track. To manipulate with his intellect, instead of letting others take from his body.

He'd learned to be useful instead of used.

But now there was hope!

She wasn't an Anhur queen, but what did it matter? There was a female in the beyond! One to serve and cherish, like he hadn't been able to do in *months*.

"Movement," Balkazar hissed, bringing their headlong sprint to a sudden halt, the war chief crouched low in the shadows.

As one, the pack inched forward. Moved away from their chosen path to peer over the edge of a deep ravine.

Ferals.

A whole horde gathered on the banks of a distant river. And from their vantage point, Sickle could see that they were massive creatures who'd grown mutated and grotesque. Each one bigger than the last. All terribly disfigured from their constant contact with the Trax virus. The infection raging, overwhelming the immune system until the host was forever changed.

Mutated and abhorrent. Utterly unrecognizable as the creatures they once were.

Something akin to sadness tugged at his soft heart, Sickle watched a battle erupt between two gargantuan beasts. Transfixed.

For a moment, it seemed as if the smaller of the two had the upper hand—and Sickle dared a tiny smile for those who'd been born disadvantaged. Seeing a message of hope, out here where hardship was the standard. Where death was easy.

But a few minor victories served only to inflate the smaller feral with overconfidence.

He got too close. Stepped inside his opponent's ridiculous reach and paid for it by taking an absolutely brutal swipe of claws to his face. Bellowing, the smaller male turned toward the watching pack. Showing them all the horrific damage wrought with one well-timed blow—one that only echoed the horrific scars marking the Alpha's once-handsome visage.

Because they were much, *much* worse than anything Sickle had ever seen.

Both eyes were obliterated, the left hanging loose on a bit of bloody cord. The right nothing more than a white smear spread over the ridge of lacerations that went clean through bone. Not quite a death blow, if the feral could survive without sight. If his gruesome wounds miraculously avoided infection.

Howling and victorious, the larger male launched a lazy attack. Jaws clamping shut about the other's wrist, he twisted his head and shattered the bones until they burst through the muscle. Gleaming in the dying light.

Sickle's mouth flooded with acid as the horde turned hungry eyes down, on one of their own who'd dared to show a glimpse of weakness.

Yipping and howling, they descended. The one who'd dealt a mortal blow the first to dine on living flesh, these ferals ate before they killed.

Horrified, Sickle couldn't look away, having only heard of such an atrocity whispered about in the darkest corners of the court gossip.

And it was with bile searing the back of his throat that Sickle watched as the ferals spread the legs of the incapacitated male. Some standing on his limbs, they worked together to ruin the fallen creature. Genitals first, a savage injury was dealt. Spilled blood visible even from this distance as the beasts roared in triumph. As the victor plunged a clawed fist into that gaping orifice and pulled slippery ropes of intestines free.

A mortal wound, and one that left the fallen male crawling to the banks of the river on his belly. Dragging the ropey ends of his guts through the mud and filth.

Sickle turned away, having already seen too much.

Having heard far more than he'd ever needed to hear.

"Filthy fucking savages," the Alpha hissed, his mane fully risen about him in a pale halo. Vibrating with disgust.

"Better they're down there eating each other," Balkazar rumbled, still watching. His face impassive even as the sounds of ripping meat echoed up from the ravine.

Silence descended upon their small pack. The only communication a fleeting glance of their eyes, and Sickle knew they were all thinking the same thing. About a certain female going into heat.

The reckless net she'd cast throughout the entire forest.

If she was unfortunate enough to get herself caught by a feral...

Well.

There would be no saving what was left.

Even if she was lucky and was taken by a feral whose lust outweighed his gluttony, she'd fall to the virus and find herself beneath the rutting hips of an entire hoard. Just another statistic no one would ever think to record.

Fingers clenching about the handle of his blade, Sickle flashed his teeth in the gloom. His cock swelled, a throbbing ache tied down and restrained behind his leathers, consumed as he was by her scent. Her slick.

"Let's go," he whispered, ears pressed flat, pointed teeth flashing in the shadows. "It's not safe for her to be alone. We have to find her. Before—"

A thick hand landed on his shoulder. The Alpha squeezed Sickle's narrow shoulder in a silent offer of comfort. "The Nine didn't send her to us just to take her away so soon," he said. "Not even they could be so cruel."

Nodding, Sickle clung to that fragile hope, falling into step when the pack moved out. On the hunt, once more.

Deep down, though, he knew—there were no gods in the beyond.

Only demons who ate without bothering to kill.

13

Heads low, the pack ran as one. Their senses saturated with the distinct and rare bouquet of slick, focused entirely on the elusive scent of breeding female where it hung heavy in the air.

The Alpha grinned, taking up the rear as he kept pace behind his pack. Pleased at how easily they meshed as a unit, all castes working together to catch their little runaway. It would be a nuisance to train her, to break her in and teach her what it was to belong to a prince's harem. But perhaps Balkazar could be tempted to take on the chore? The Alpha had never been fond of teary virgins, and the war chief had earned a reward. The chance to mold her tight slit to his knot.

She'd been running, that much the Alpha knew for certain. It was the undeniable taste of adrenaline laced through the trees, married to her scent. In the way her footprints had lengthened when they were visible in the fluffy loam lining the forest floor.

Bristling, a low growl erupted from between his lips, making Sickle startle, a yelp wrenched from the Hathorian's throat. And sending a wide-eyed glance over his shoulder, Sickle's shoulders hunched while he ran. Cringing.

It was an instinctive thing, Sickle's reaction.

That of *prey*.

A lowly Omega who knew his place without having to learn a hard lesson, the way this female did not.

Baring his teeth at the small male, the Alpha found cause to be furious with Sickle's entire species. With this Omega female for putting herself in danger, when she should have come to him and begged for his knot.

It was the way of things. Already he could imagine the satisfaction of it. Of seeing her pregnant yet available, grateful for the opportunity to breed for them...

Snarling, he barked orders at their backs. *Faster. Harder.* "Bring that little bitch to me!"

He needn't have bothered.

Each male knew the taste of her, now. All had drunk deep of the creek laced with her need. Her slick.

A precious thing he'd never have shared with common hybrids before his exile.

But... *now*?

He was no longer a prince. Docked.

Baring horrific scars as proof of his failure. Who was he to stand over lesser males? To deny them the one thing that could bind them all closer together?

What did it matter, anyway? She was just a breeder.

No matter how perfectly she'd gripped his knot as he bred her, nor how tight the seal, she was not an Anhur female. She was a tool to induce rut, no more or less than the cock she'd tried to carve to relieve herself. An Omega. She could give him an army of hybrid sons to defend his territory, but only an Anhur female could give him a legacy.

If she'd been a member of his species, things would have been different. He and Balkazar would fight to the death to claim a female who could give them *that*.

But a breeder? One whose sole purpose was to give pleasure and create warriors? To induce rut and beg for more. The Alpha was glad for the chance to see her stretched by his pack, to reward his new brothers for their hard work. Even if the hybrids were sterile, they would punish her with their girth and length alone. Her innocent sheath would be trained by hybrid cocks, for only the Anhur could offer a proper knot.

What did it matter if the kits whelped from the girl were his or Balkazar's?

The war chief was content in his place as second, but giving him a few hybrid brats was an easy way to buy Balkazar's obedience and eternal loyalty.

Growling low in his throat, the Alpha leapt over a fallen tree, almost landing on Sickle's heels.

The dainty thing was beginning to flag, his stamina sorely tested against superior males. And yet, with a toothy grimace, Sickle forced one foot ahead of the other, his breaths coming in great, heaving swallows. It was the first time the Alpha had seen him this animated, this engaged, no matter the pain of denial.

Teeth bared, unable to quit or surrender, Sickle's body would fight the hardest to claim something he could never really have, for the girl would belong to an Anhur, *first*.

In the distance, came the echo of a pained cry. A single, haunting wail that echoed through the forest.

Without being told, the pack renewed their charge. Not a word spoken between males who knew just what sort of danger lurked in the beyond.

And then Balkazar skidded to a halt, the war chief standing with feet spread, his hackles rising in a great cloud of fury. Clenched fist held aloft in a silent command for them to halt immediately—a command not even the Alpha dared rebuke. No matter the consequences.

"*Priiigussss...*" came a hissing rattle, the

voice distorted by the rumble of a phlegmy growl.

An eerie sound that made the Alpha bristle with a dominant, yet hesitant shiver.

The war chief flicked two fingers of his raised fist, signaling them to tighten their ranks. To protect the weakest and prepare for bloodshed. His hackles, too, were standing tight and high. Muscles shivering with restraint.

Frozen on the cusp of action, the pack went utterly still. Six pairs of eyes focused on a single figure ambling through the brush.

A feral infected with the Trax virus.

Stripped naked and rolled in filth. His skin bore the marks of a loner who'd been challenged and lost, his shoulders were raw and bloody where he was ravaged by the hardships of the wild.

Freshly infected and showing the early signs of his long, slow demise, he was already touched by the grotesque physical mutation the Trax virus was infamous for causing. But only *just*.

They'd been too late to save him.

His wounds still wept, showing how fresh the infection really was. That the pack had been mere *days* away from adding this loner to their ranks, instead of being forced to put him down.

Oblivious to the watchful eyes, the infected male ground his teeth. Head slung low, skin stretched thin where the bone of his forehead bulged. Deformed. Already making him utterly unrecognizable as the proud Anhur he'd once been.

Hanging from slack lips, a drop of grayish drool glistened and swayed, until it snapped. Spattering the leaf litter. He stopped then, tugging at a thick bulge.

His prick—or what was left of it.

The thing being tortured between clawed fingers would no longer meet the definition of a sex organ. Bloated and raw, it was a mess of boils and hardening patches of bright red skin. Where the blood had been forced too close to the surface for too long, unable to drain. And from the tip, yellow semen dribbled with each pass of pumping fist.

Mindless, he'd been drawn in by the scent of slick. Rotten brain retaining nothing but the most basic instincts, to eat, drink, and fuck.

This feral was hunting.

And though his gait was slow and ambling, he would pursue their Hathorian female until his dying brain lost the trail, or he was presented with an obstacle he could not overcome.

Silent, the Alpha crept through the ranks of his pack, taking his place on step ahead of the war chief. His gaze settling on the infected male who paused to sniff at the trunk of a young tree.

"*For Priiigussss...*" the feral moaned, voice thick with arousal and a hint of despair, pausing only to tug at his weeping cock. Shoulders bunching and coiled as he worked himself into a lather. Head thrown back, they watched his face contort. Cheeks flushed, eyes glassy, hair matted with acrid sweat and arousal—yet above it all, the unfortunate creature reeked of sickness.

Of disease.

The Alpha sneered, unabashedly watching another male as he shivered and came, spilling rank and curdled cream. The muscles of his ass flexing just below a ragged wound where his tail had once stood high and proud, the feral turned his back. Returning to the hunt after marking a tree the girl had touched.

Claiming it—*her*.

It could not be allowed.

The female was *his*.

Taking a deep breath, the Alpha issued a bellow of challenge that shattered the silence. The pack fanned out around him, forming a semi-circle around their prey.

Not so much as a startled blink was given in reaction, the feral mindlessly pursing their female's scent, repeating, "*Priiigussss...*" over and over again under his breath. A mantra none could comprehend.

"What's that mean, you think?" Balkazar asked, brows drawn together in a tight scowl.

The Alpha shrugged, feeling the ghost of his tail flick in agitation. Indecisive, for in terms of physical, mental, and battle prowess, their pack was proven. Blooded even before the hybrids had joined their ranks and pledged their strength.

This threat was inconsequential.

But should any of them touch that infected creature...

It was Sickle who stepped forward. The little male in full blower, his muscles held so taut, they vibrated as he faced off against a thing that could doom him with a single, rotten touch.

"Sickle," Balkazar warned and placed a large hand on a slight shoulder.

Ignoring a direct command from the war chief, Sickle shook off the heavy touch and stepped forward. Bristling. Saliva dripping from pointed teeth as his slender chest vibrated in a low growl. His ears laid out, not tucked back in submissive fear, but displaying uncharacteristic anger. Challenge.

He too, was ignored by the feral.

Until the wind changed.

Carrying Sickle's scent—that of an enraged Hathorian—a gentle breeze ruffled fur matted with blood and filth. Pausing in the middle of whispering, "*For Priiigusss...*" the feral male stopped short. Head rotating on a twitching pike, the feral turned glassy eyes upon Sickle. Spent cock twitching to renewed life.

Sickle grinned through his madness, issuing a delicate roar of his own.

And then he lunged.

With a flick of his dainty, Hathorian wrist, a blade shot forth. Flashing in the fading light, faster than the charging infected. It landed with a decisive thunk, one that seemed to register long after the blade had stuck its mark.

And for a moment, they were frozen in a tableau. Sickle holding the pose exactly the way Balkazar had told him. The infected still, brow folding in gentle, almost innocent confusion.

Wheezing once, the feral male whistled high at the back of his throat. Foggy eyes going wide. His hand—missing two and a half fingers—clutched at the steel protruding from the base of his windpipe. Dislodging it just enough to let the blood really flow, drowning out any sound that was leaking from a ruined voice box.

He fell before it could be worked free, the watching pack gathered as the creature breathed its last. Lips moving around a wet, "*Priiigussss,*" he soaked the detritus in gushing crimson.

Huffing, Sickle adjusted his sweat-damp hair, then took a step toward his victim.

"Leave it," the Alpha barked, large hand clapping over a slender shoulder. Stopping him in place with a heavy scowl.

"But my knife—"

The war chief stepped between the Hathorian and the corpse and said,

"Shouldn't have thrown it if you wanted to keep it. You know the rules. No exposure."

"But—"

"Look at him," the Alpha snapped, stepping around Balkazar. Forcing Sickle's eyes to land on the thing that had once been a proud Anhur. "Is that what you want, boy? Hmm? To be put down and left to rot instead of given to the fires? Unable to go into the arms of the Nine?"

It was Sickle's turn to scowl, and he did it in such a way that the Alpha had to struggle not to laugh. "Of course not," Sickle spat. "Leaving a blade behind is wasteful. That's all I meant."

Indulging the fancy little thing, the Alpha offered a gruff smile. "I'll have a new one forged for you once we've claimed this girl."

Sickle rolled his eyes, but relented. Going where he was led.

"We're getting close," Balkazar said, keeping their pace slow. Sedate. Following the sweet, teasing trail of slick—ears primed for any hint that there may be more infected roaming these woods. Tense, right down to the hairs bristling along his nape, Balkazar appeared cautious as he navigated through the wood. Looking for the minuscule signs that her passage was recent, that the trails of hand-painted slick where converging in some semblance of logic.

Impatient, the Alpha pushed aside some dense, hanging foliage, and the forest ended.

Revealing a barren clearing complete with a three-tiered hot spring, and what looked to be a rocky hillock with a sheer face of red stone.

"My prince," Balkazar hissed, seizing his arm and trying to slow his pace.

The Alpha shook him off, hackles raised. His attention caught by the logistics of this oasis.

Defensible, fresh water supply, secluded. It was a perfect little knoll, one the Alpha could see himself—

He stepped on something that snapped. Something that crunched underfoot.

In an instant, his field of vision flipped as he was hauled off his feet in less time than it took to blink. Breath torn from his chest with the sheer velocity in which he was snatched up. Limbs askew, he thrashed, looking for the attacker—blinded by defensive rage. Snarling, sinking his teeth into the nearest warm flesh, he clamped down. Slashing and howling, drawing blood.

Balkazar's scent spilled thick and cloying. Familiar. *Anhur*.

A threat.

Blood rushed into the Alpha's mouth, igniting his murky, testosterone clouded brain with a spark of pure rage. Blood lust rising hot and fast, he shook his head. Driving his teeth straight into the muscle. Deep as they could go. Instinct taking hold, he was triggered by the coppery tang rushing over his tongue.

A roar pounded at his ear drums. The body of the other male writhing beneath his weight, fighting when he should have relented. Submitted. Instead, he rose to the occasion, challenging a Karahmet prince for breeding rights.

Insolence would be addressed with lethal judgment.

"Stop!"

Though shrill, the shout was loud enough to be heard over the scream of deadly instinct, loud enough to drown out the smell of testosterone fogging up the Alpha's brain.

Sickle. The dainty Hathorian stood below them, alone at the forest's edge.

"It's a trap," Sickle said, liquid brown eyes ringed in white. "She set a trap."

The Alpha blinked.

Blinked again, releasing his hold on the other male's shoulder. Teeth leaving a distinct ring.

A trap.

That clever little bitch had set a trap. He'd stepped on a hair trigger and was ensnared in a hand-crafted net which would yield to no amount of snarling or struggling. Not giving under the weight of two furious Anhur males drunk on pheromones and rut, whose limbs were now tangled around *each other*. Both of them bloodied and speckled with the other's teeth.

One by one, each member of their pack had been caught up by the breeder's whims.

Konjo hung to their left, upside down. Alone, yet breathing hard as if he too had struggled to right himself. Pupils tiny dots of nothing as he strained to free himself and reach the female who'd saturated them in her scent. Who'd shamed them all without so much as bothering to make herself seen.

Behind them, Keever and Micah had been snapped up together. Micah, whose dark skin bore the raised keloid scars that spoke of his dedication to battle. Deadly and massive, Micah fought his capture the hardest. Snapping and bellowing his impotent rage, trying to pull the rope lattice apart with nothing but sheer, physical prowess—no matter the danger he posed to Keever.

"Stop fighting!" Sickle shouted, trying to get the attention of the hybrids writhing in their bonds. "I'll cut you down, if you'll just give me a moment—"

But Sickle didn't have a blade. It was protruding from the windpipe of the diseased creature he'd slain. Abandoned.

Shooting a helpless glance up, Sickle grimaced. Wise enough not to voice his judgment, long schooled in the art of quiet reprimand in his service to the Anhur queens. Instead, he traced the anchor keeping them suspended with sharp eyes. Tracing the actions of a female lost to her hormones, he searched for the place she'd anchored the ropes.

Silence fell upon the wood. An eerie shiver skated over the Alpha's skin, making his hackles bristle, his claws extend.

"Hurry," he hissed, scanning the clearing for anything out of place.

And so it was that he was the first to see her. The only one who saw the lone figure rise from dark waters thick with misty steam.

14

Shivering, the girl stood. Twitching, overheated muscles quivering as she paused at the water's edge, drawn in by the sound of furious shouting.

Hadim.

He'd come for her at last.

A tremor skated through her system, revulsion and lust all rolled into one. Her hatred had only grown since she'd last seen her master, and now, absent her shield of clothing, she could see what he really was. The almost deadly reminder etched into the flesh of her right arm, four claws that had torn deep enough to never fade.

She could see him just there, struggling in the nets. Ruined face pinched in a tight scowl, another male sharing his dangling prison. Caught in nets she'd woven herself.

Fingers snaking down, she touched the smoldering, liquid heat streaming between her legs. The lips of her sex plump and wet with the ache of need. Her glands rubbing together with every throbbing pulse of her heart.

The males fell silent. Quiet enough to hear her fingers squelch when she pulled them free.

Watching.

She took another few hesitant steps toward her prize, water splashing around her thighs.

The entire pack. Instead of two manageable, sterile hybrid males, she'd caught all three. Caught both Hadim *and* his war chief. All dangling in her nets unable to fight their way free.

Except one.

Sickle.

The Hathorian male who hadn't been ravaged by the others. One who was still aesthetic perfection, despite a certain cautious rugged edge that was beginning to peek through the smoky glamour. Maybe because of it.

Tipping her head back, she tasted the still air. Slick spilling down her thighs as she stepped over the edge of the hot spring.

Hadim had often threatened to share her with his favorite sons. Promised to stretch her out until her *Biquea* gland grew hardened and stubborn, until they couldn't be subdued without two knots ripping her up at once.

Heat spilled down her nape, sending her muscles into a fresh wave of scalding spasm.

Heat that pulled and clenched. Pulsing where it couldn't throb. Oozing where it ached the most.

Where she needed to be stuffed with her master's thick cream until the burning need faded away and she was fat with a litter of Hadim's hybrids...

Hips rolling, she mewled. Feet moving of their own volition, nipples begging to be caught and pinched. Twisted until they went red.

"Purple," she moaned, panting as she stumbled toward them. "Make them purple..."

"Look for wounds, Sickle," one of the males hissed, his voice laced with warning. One of the Anhur males, who had what she needed. Who might have been the Alpha. *Her* Alpha. "She may be infected, you can't—" He seemed to choke on the words, his voice dissolving into a guttural snarl that made her gush, wishing that sound had been breathed against her ear. Into her hair.

Above and inside.

"Don't fucking touch her, Sickle!" Hadim hissed, his ruined face twisted with rage. Unrecognizable as the master she'd once known. "She's *mine*."

Flashing blunt teeth, she tugged on a lock of jet-black, *loose* hair. Showing them all what she'd done. "No braids," she whispered, speech slurred. Her words drawing confused side-eyed glances from all but *him*. Hadim.

"You *know*," she hissed, ears flat, sneaking quick shifty glances at the scarred visage scowling from above. "You like braids best," she explained and shook her head. When she grinned, it was with ears laid out to the sides. Coy, as she said, "Not for you."

And with a careless flick of her wrist, she pushed sheets of sopping wet hair over her shoulder. Fingers tangled in the snarls, she exposed herself to a pack of males who were not her master. A crime that would see them all dismembered in the Silver City.

But here?

Her arousal surged with the thrill of disobedience. With reckless glee. And for the length of time it took for a bead of water to trace her skin—starting at her collarbone and bumping over and between swollen breasts—she held them rapt and still with nothing but her nude presence.

Even Sickle, who was unbound. Who could have taken everything, for although he was indeed a dainty little thing, he was male. Strong in ways a pampered harem slave would never be.

But not strong enough to resist a female in need.

Maybe he could do the job? It was a risk to allow another of her species to touch her, certainly, but what else had she to do, but spend the rest of the month searching for Yarrow root to cleanse the filth from her womb? Besides, she'd never had a Hathorian male...

Never even seen one.

And it would be the sweetest kind of revenge to have her first in front of Hadim...

She approached gracefully, balanced on the balls of her feet when she could manage not to stumble. Mindful of the dips and eddies carved into slick red stone, except when the impact from each step shook a droplet of slick loose. Distracting, for it spattered as far down as the elegant bones of her ankles—so much that she began to worry about the safety of it all.

Surely, to produce... so... so *much* wasn't healthy?

A high-pitched whine crawled up the back of her throat, her fingers snaking down to disappear between the folds of her puffy lips once more. It had been days of frustration and slippery wanting. Days of endless fretting while she fought with everything she had. Picturing Hadim's handsome face as she fucked herself with a wooden cock, cursing his entire bloodline when all she could think without wishing he was covering her back and forcing her to take more than she could.

Worst of all, it was her first time going into heat without the aid of suppressors. And without anything to keep her hormones in check, she'd have no choice, but to abandon higher reasoning altogether.

Utterly, and on an epic scale.

For this was only the beginning. A precursor. Only a taste of how bad this natural season would get once it was truly upon her... once the need to breed set in, her eggs made to drop.

She was already lost.

Couldn't stop.

Frozen in place, Sickle seemed unable to move as she approached. The glamorous male watching her hips roll with wide, white-rimmed eyes.

He really was beautiful—more than she was, certainly. Across his hairline blue ink dappled and twisted. His lips plush pillows, cheekbones giving his profile an ethereal cast that made her both nervous and giddy. Skin clear and smooth, except for the tiny dimples that showed where he'd been pierced with jewels on golden posts, the gems no longer his to display. By the Nine, his eyes were the *exact* shade of the sweet syrup Hadim had put in her tea as a reward for a pleasing breeding.

No matter how beautiful he was, Sickle was not strictly... feminine. Where she was slender to the point of fragile—wrists, ankles, neck—his bones were noticeably thicker. Solid, where she was not. They'd lived similar lives, both being slaves to their Anhur counterpart, but his frame carried more muscle. Taller and broader than her, but once she was standing close enough to taste his breath, she knew they'd fit together.

An obvious, natural match.

"Take it off," she rasped, cheeks hot. Reaching out to touch the swell of that plump bottom lip. To press trembling forefinger in, to paint his tongue with slick.

Sickle lurched into action, his eyes turning black as he raced to comply. Suckling at her finger as he bared his skin to her ravenous gaze.

One of the Anhur bellowed, the tone of authority making her knees tremble for just a moment. A command she couldn't decipher, for though she gushed, she didn't spare Hadim even the slightest glance.

There was a naked Hathorian quivering in the chilly breeze. The head of his modest cock purple with need, dripping and pulsing, and yet he did not move. Wide eyes fixated on her *and nothing else*. Ignoring the rising chorus demanding that he check her for wounds. That she could be infected...

Sickle kicked off the last of his clothing, only to stop and stand before her with luminous eyes. Waiting.

Her breath hitched, unaccustomed to being obeyed. To a male who did as she asked, then stood still. Ready for the next command.

It was a marvel.

One she would savor for the precious gift that it was.

Mouth watering, she circled. Each booming Anhur command echoed through her ribs, blending into the next. Serving no purpose, except to make her salivate for a Hathorian male. For the taboo rush that flooded her veins, she disobeyed Hadim for the first time in her life.

Far as she could see, Sickle hadn't been damaged or used for his pleasure. There was no scent of stale seed on his skin and no bruises marking his hips where rough, careless fingers might have found purchase in abuse. Even his tail stump had been well cared for and had healed over much better than hers.

With each circling step around her prey, her thighs squished the gooey petals of her pussy lips together. Mashing that little bean and sending slick to speckle the red rock underfoot.

There was a certain element of justice to give Sickle a taste in full view of Hadim, who could easily win any version of competition against the Hathorians. Something sweet to find satisfaction with her kind while the others were made to watch. Made to strain against their bonds and bark their impotent commands.

Grinning, she lapped at the back of Sickle's neck—just above the top of a tattoo she knew marked his lineage, for hers looked the same. Thrilled by the way he flinched, but allowed her access to fill her lungs with his scent. Familiarizing herself.

Gaze trickling down, over the lithe bumps of his abs, she made eye contact with the slit of his cock. It wept for her attention, burping up pearls of glistening temptation too great to deny.

She dropped without thinking, knees striking the red stone. The brief flare of pain gobbled up by the hormones switching the wires in her brain. Crossing pleasure with pain until a drop of slick slipped free, reaching to connect her clasping, empty cunt with the sunbaked earth. A pearly strand shimmering in the sunlight.

"You first," she mumbled.

Then swallowed him whole.

15

She was on him before he could muster the dexterity to speak a single word. Engulfing his length all the way to the back of her throat, only to swallow when she got there. Tight ring of cartilage kneading at his engorged head.

Yelping, Sickle's hips flexed, pumping a single rope of excitement down her throat. Painting the back of her tongue when he withdrew with a gasp.

"So warm," he groaned, seizing a handful of silky black hair. Forcing her to look at him, even though all he wanted was for her to swallow his load before his brothers took their fill. "Please," he said, voice slipping into the shivery dulcet tones the queens had loved so much. "I... I need to taste..."

Something flashed across her face. Either wonder or anguish, he couldn't rightly say. Only that it was something of great depth before it was shuttered away on her next blink.

The mysterious, dark-eyed beauty smiled then, but it was toothy and wild. Her blunted teeth creating a painful ache in his chest, a great surge of pity for the little female. Unwarranted, for she was savage enough to make him shiver with want, to make his balls clench where they were held tight and close to his body. Preparing to unload everything he had.

Grinning, the girl tugged him down. Guided him to lay on his back so she could crawl up and over. Pinning him between naked thighs, she hooked her legs about his shoulders and straddled his chest—the petals of a swollen, glistening slit on lewd display.

Above them, the pack howled. Demanding to be set free so they might seed her first.

Take what he was being given.

Something... defiant came over Sickle then. Something that demanded he breed this little bitch in the old ways. In front of the pack, so they might see the sticky evidence of his claim.

Growling low in his throat, he wrapped both arms around her thighs, spreading her wider. Embracing this chance while it was his to do with as he pleased.

This was what he'd been trained for. All the years of abuse and denial were for *this* moment. For her. To use lips, teeth, tongue, and fingers until she was quaking above him.

Until she'd left him bruised and dripping in want.

He buried his face between her thighs, using the flat of his tongue to lap up as much slick as he could get, before diving deeper. Going inside to drink straight from the source.

Ecstasy singed his taste buds. Burning with every swallow, her taste left him ravaged. His throat parched and dry, flexing with the need to gulp her down and soothe his aches with nothing but the slick ambrosia pouring from a needy little cunt.

It was her turn to whine. Her turn to tremble and quake, for taking a position of dominance was as unnatural to a Hathorian female as submission was to an Anhur.

Sickle knew it all too well.

To need and not know how to ask. To give, knowing nothing would be returned.

Just as Sickle had never been chosen first, and the Alpha had never been told to wait, so too could he assume this girl had never been allowed to ask.

Tearing one hand from his grip on her hip, Sickle moved to cup a breast. Catching the rosy point between forefinger and thumb, he rolled it across the first knuckle just to make her gasp. To watch her face contort.

"P-purple," she gasped, clapping her hand over his. Showing him how to pinch until the tip of her breast began to bloom with color.

She'd chosen well for her first. Of them all, Sickle had enough girth to spread her without causing pain. To stretch her delicate flesh around his knot, while allowing her to focus solely on her own pleasure. He was the safe option. The weakest male... Hathorian.

But she had chosen him.

Pulling her clit between his teeth, he worried at that engorged bean. Suckling until she mewled for him to stop. Until she was so sensitive, she flinched at his every breathy exhale. Overstimulated by design, for Sickle had been trained to please.

And he applied every trick he'd ever learned.

Growling into her, he delighted in the flexing muscles caught in his palms. That she squirmed and bucked, trying to get away and get closer from one second to the next. Fueled by the breathy little squeals he drew from her throat, as her knees shifted on the stone beneath his head, she rode his face. Seeking her peak.

Above it all, the pack howled their demands that went unheard by the two Hathorians filling the clearing with the scent of wet heat.

Lapping at her clit once more, Sickle tried to bring her off.

"No," she gasped and lurched back. Breaking his grip, she slid fragile fingers around his, and pulled until he released her. Utterly shameless, she sat on his chest—

leaving his skin wet with the evidence of her arousal—and straightened her legs. Giving him a direct view of a gorgeous ripe pussy and tiny flexing ass hole.

Sickle swallowed, hard. Almost grateful when she shifted again, planted her knees beneath his armpits, then shimmied back. Braced above him on all fours, she was left exposed. Displaying that perfect, wet slit to the bound males made to watch, yet every ounce of Sickle's attention had narrowed to the spot where the head of his dick nudged something hot and moist. Straining and sliding between her cheeks.

Stooping, she set her nose to the spot just beneath his chin, then licked at his pulse. Where his flavor would be strongest.

"What's your name?" he asked, desperately needing to blink. Terrified to miss even a single instant.

Her head tilted, a frown pinching the skin between her brows.

And it was then, as she stared into his eyes with a foggy, confused glare, that he realized just how far gone this little female really was. Pupils blown wide, cheeks flushed, her forehead damp with a sheen of dew—he wasn't altogether certain she'd understood the question.

Perhaps it was her first time? Her first heat?

It would explain the confusion, but not the rest of it. The defiance. The traps.

He'd never seen such a thing happen to the Anhur queens. Never, during all the years he'd served, had he seen a queen so lost to her needs.

So... helpless.

Sickle groaned, unable to speak even as he reached for her hips. Trying to push her lower, to fit himself between her thighs and add to the mess dripping into his neatly groomed pubic hair.

To have a creature so soft, so vulnerable at his mercy? Not even the arms of the Nine could be so precious. Surely his ancestors watched from the ashes, weeping dusty tears of joy to see him this way.

All sharp lines and delicate curves, she was fine boned. Elegant, yet sharp. A high-born specimen, meant to whelp only the best offspring for her master.

And now she belonged to the pack.

Sickle paused only to send his cock through her sodden folds. Once, twice, three times—lubricating himself to the tone of better males demanding he stop. Grimacing, he crooned as she sank down, swallowing his pole to the root. Sheets of sodden, jet-black hair hung between them. Dripping. Begging to be wrapped around his fist.

"So tight," Sickle hummed, eyes rolling back. "Don't worry," he rasped. "I'll make it" —a breathy grunt—"it'll be good for your first time, pet."

A breathy laugh whispered above him,

but her glands shuddered around his prick. Bearing down, he flexed his hips as she picked up a delightful, selfish rhythm. Sickle thrust as deep as he could, then held stiff. Offering her every spare inch of dick he possessed, even as he pulled her down. As he set his nose to the junction between jaw and the slender column of her throat. Inhaling deep, intimate breaths. Lips catching her taste.

One hand buried in her hair, the other locked onto the meat of her left hip, Sickle forced her to ride. To grind her swollen little bean into his pelvis and ignore the other males.

Slick squelched out around his base, soaking his nuts.

She was tightening around him. Each pass of her hips bringing her closer to climax, the tight fit enticing his knot to swell. An urge he fought.

Eyes squeezed shut, Sickle gripped her hip as hard as he could. Keeping her folded over him as he bred her, nose pressed to throat. His mouth watered with the urge to mark her in the way of their people. Her nipples scraping over his chest.

And then her *Biquea* glands pulsed against his shaft. Working in tandem, they kneaded and milked. Tiny gripping hands forcing his knot to bloom even before he spilled all that frothy seed, expanding against her glands at just the right moment to send her spiraling into bliss.

Twitching and quivering, he felt her orgasm ripple around him. Felt her glands clench and chew on his shaft as he fought to subdue her. The pleasure from so fine an intimate grip sent him into convulsions of ecstasy he was ill-prepared to deal with, let alone weather. Pumping jet after jet of seed into her sodden channel, only to seal it inside with his knot.

Fighting against the pulse of glands too tight to deflate.

When he was finally spent, his sack drained and hanging limp between tacky thighs, he tried to purr for her. To show his gratitude for that short and wild ride by producing a frail little warble high in his chest.

She shivered, bearing down. Still clenching. Still riding him, and though he'd begun to soften, he could still feel her glands locked around his knot. Defiantly hard. Filled to the brim with the antidote to so mindless a season.

An antidote he'd failed to extract.

As he met the inky gaze of a female consumed by need, he knew she hadn't been tamed.

Knew she needed more.

Tears sprang to his eyes, but with a tight swallow, Sickle pushed her off. Withdrawing from her warmth with a sucking pop.

There was nothing for it. The others had to be freed.

His queen needed, and he would provide.

16

Eyes bleary, womb seeded but still aching, she watched the blurry form walk away from her. Leaving her throbbing and hot.

Empty and too full.

"Nooo..." she mewled, trying to crawl after him. Skinning her knees, her palms. Ass swaying as globs of cream and slick spilled from flush, plump lips. Long strings of pearly white reached for the red rock, staining it a deep, murderous red where it dripped and dropped. "Please... *please...*"

But Sickle ignored her. Walking faster than she could crawl, she watched him approach the other males. The dangerous ones who wouldn't let her control the pace. Who wouldn't obey, and couldn't relate to her on a fundamental level—the way only another Hathorian could.

Sickle abandoned her without a backward glance. A shard of red stone clutched tight in his hand, and even through the fog, she knew what he intended to do. That his loyalties lay with his masters, not his people.

A hiss spattered between her lips, through blunted teeth. Ears pressed flat to her skull, she tried to reverse. To crawl back into her den and hide before it was too late... before she forgot why she should deny the burning need to be stretched out by a thick knot when they were ready and available. Just as needy as her.

"Let us down," one of the Anhur snarled. Commanding and deep, though she couldn't tell which had spoken. Hadim or his war chief.

She gushed, hardly understanding the language when Sickle said, "The ropes are... well made." He cleared his throat. "I-I'm trying, sir."

And he was.

Blinking lazy and doe-eyed, the female watched Sickle work to saw through the anchor ropes for the first of her three hanging nets. His lips moving in a constant flood of words she could neither hear nor understand.

All she could do was watch. Clenching around nothing—trying to tear her eyes away as the seconds dwindled. Would they let her live after what she'd done? After she'd chosen a Hathorian over them?

Hadim wouldn't.

Her twisted, fuck-drunk brain could only

hope they'd knot her properly before she died. That she might have a few stolen moments of relief before she went into the arms of the Nine.

Cursing, Sickle tried to rush through the last few strands, but it snapped before he finished.

With a startled yelp, a net fell from the trees.

And when she could focus, the girl could see only *one* figure fighting to get free. Not the Anhur, then, but a hybrid.

He was up before she could lift her head, eyes blazing. Bigger than an Anhur by at least a third, the massive male closed the space between them in three loping strides. He scooped her into his arms without bothering to slow, snarling but a single word. "*Konjo.*"

His name.

Helpless to resist, she squealed. Her sex convulsing with renewed tension, delighted by the savage absence of this male submitting to the rut. A wild-thing, unleashed. All hers. The hybrid she'd come to claim.

Konjo surprised her, for instead of tossing her down and stuffing her full, he dropped her in the same spot Sickle had bred her. The pool of cooling liquids squished against her skin when he pinned her spine to the earth. Folded her knees to her chest, spreading her wide and vulnerable. Head dipping between soiled thighs, he took a sip straight from the wellspring of two satisfied Hathorians.

Tasting Sickle's salty spend even as he drank deep of slick.

Nothing so filthy had ever turned her on more as watching this strange male lap at her pussy. Nothing so raunchy as knowing he couldn't help but drink the spending that was both male and female, that he was lost to instinct.

Just as she was.

But when he set his lips to that little knot of tension and sucked her clit into his mouth, everything resembling sentient thoughts evaporated. Exhaled on a breathy groan, forgotten in an instant.

Hips bucking, pinned and helpless beneath a male heavier than she by an absurd margin, she gasped. Hovering right on the edge of climax, yet needing something a little more—

Konjo plunged two thick fingers into seeded quim, utterly void of anything even similar to finesse, and finger-fucked her. Making her juices ooze and burp around his digits, he sent her eyes rolling back. Made her back arch.

When it happened, she hadn't the faculties to warn him. Could hardly understand what it was, much less think to say something. No, instead, she soaked his face and forearms. Screaming as she squirted all over the hybrid.

Grinning, Konjo didn't stop. Gave her no other option but to take it as he milked her

sheath for every shuddering breath of pleasure it could give.

Her only response was to grunt and flop,
fucking his fingers as she rode out her climax
—and the next one after it. Pinching her nipples until the little beads turned blue from
the abuse. Almost perfect.

Konjo, it seemed, couldn't help himself
after that.

And when next the wild female opened
her eyes, it was with a gasp—for she'd been
filled with every inch of Konjo's thick cock in
a single, well-lubricated thrust.

He spared nothing for elegance. Gave her
no room to adjust, he merely began to rut.
Hard and fast, he fucked her into the stone.
Pressing her knees into her collarbones as he
lost himself. Eyes glassy. Thighs slapping her
cheeks, he emptied her of Sickle's sperm,
dragging it from her depths with the anvil
scraping her insides clean. Making room for
seed that wouldn't grow.

Pausing only to snarl at the wind, as a
starving wolf over a wasted carcass.

Almost unable to draw breath, she settled
in to weather it. Just as she'd done whenever
Hadim had been in a savage mood. Knowing
at this pace, it wouldn't be long before the
rutting hybrid filled and knotted her. That
the sparkle of oxygen deprivation would do
nothing but heighten her climax when it
came.

Hadim had taught her that, too.

Sweat spattered her forehead as Konjo scrambled for better purchase. Driving himself deeper, he forced her cervix to draw back. To make room for the blunt and pounding tool spreading her sodden folds.

Something tightened in her lower back, tracing the edge of her pelvic cradle. Internal muscles growing tight, her glands more and more turgid. Pulsing in agony, even as they tried to clasp at a knot. That delicious contradiction sending her into pre-spasms that saw her eyes rolling back. Delighting in the bruising grip marking the backs of her knees as Konjo held her spread and open.

"Come—" he snarled, teeth snapping just above her throat, close enough for the threat to break her concentration and derail what was promising to be a powerful climax. "I'm coming. Ugh! Take it, you filthy Omega bitch. Take it all!" he bellowed, dropping into her one final time, so deep he managed to nudge her cervix and splash his spending across that tightly puckered entrance to her womb.

Spurt after hot, salty spurt Konjo forced into her depths, each blast sprayed deeper with a mighty flex of his ass cheeks. Rocking tight and messy through her channel.

When his defunct sperm began to overflow, the Beta's knot expanded at last, but given the length of the cock bruising her guts, it wasn't half the knot she was expecting. Sleek and long, where Sickle had been thick and wide. Konjo wasn't capable of stopping his weak cream from trickling between the globes of her pale cheeks, much less forcing her *Biquea* glands into submission.

And yet he continued to pump her full, spilling globs of harmless seed.

Ears pressed flat, she waited for the trembling male to ease off a little so she could take a breath.

Konjo collapsed with a final grunt, dripping sweat across her brow as he panted. Forehead bumping her collarbone, he freed her right thigh, letting her heel find purchase on the now slippery stone. Crushing her. Fingertips absently toying with her nipples.

She hissed at him, setting flimsy nails against his flushed pectorals. Causing him to jerk, both inside and out. His prick kicking to life once more.

But she was no blushing innocent. She was a harem slave. Knowledgeable and trained in the way of pleasing rutting males, no matter that she'd never had a hybrid before—they were all the same. Knot or not.

Shifting most of her weight into her right heel, she thrust beneath him, at first, doing nothing but giving the impression that she wanted more. That her slick flowed just for him.

When she began to move—writhing and pushing—the hybrid male discovered what it was to fuck one of his mother's people.

His eyes rolled back, showing the whites in a grotesque ring. One that made her gag and sweat as the past surged to the fore, clouding her vision with a fine mist.

Beloved blue eyes rolling. Lurching. Left one twitching as it stuttered in the socket. A garish, fleshy mask slid over the kind face she'd loved, now forever still. Fucking hideous and wrong. A mask that sagged, smiling around a gaping, sucking maw...

Head spinning, she yelped. Ears lying flat, teeth bared. Clenched. Adrenaline flooded her system, every wild thrash of her heart inching her closer to flat-out panic. Her vision split between reality and horror.

Fetid breath misted her cheeks, fleshy jowls quivering above her as the beast wearing a beloved mask became lost to the rut. Grunting as it speared into her guts, it burbled up red foam that reeked of spoiled seed. Long strings of drool reaching for her face... her lips. Alive and wriggling, trying to worm down her throat... to burrow into her womb...

Pupils blown out, she reacted. Pure instinct fueled by unresolved terror, giving her strength she'd never had. Strength she wouldn't remember the instant it faded and burned out. With one foot planted on red rocks, she bucked beneath him. Lithe and deceptively strong, she forced that living nightmare to roll then settled astride it, balanced on a spear of throbbing power. Her left knee trapped in a massive hand, the other braced against a thick, sweat-slicked chest.

Scrubbing at her eyes with the heel of her

palm, she tried to banish the repulsive thing beneath her, then dared a peek.

Still grinning, the grotesque creature writhed between her hips. Thrashed and bucked until its head struck the earth with a hollow thud. Her own hand flashed out, claws sunk into waxy dead flesh. Pulling the meat apart with hardly any effort, her fingers coming away sticky with unspeakable gore. And there, where the voice box should have been, thick arteries and veins spraying clotted jam that never stopped gushing... Through it all, the beast laughed as it fucked her from below. Dealt a mortal blow, and still battering her cervix harder than the savage grip bruising her hips... Still denying her a knot...

Using everything she'd ever learned beneath Hadim's pounding hips, she again squeezed her eyes shut. Blocking out the ghastly creature making a mess between her thighs. Tears streaking down flushed and dirty cheeks, she flexed her pelvic floor. Trembling with the effort to crush that slimy shaft with an insufficient knot, to capture it in the tight band of swollen tissue it couldn't compress.

Her *Biquea* glands cinched tight and held fast, drawing an inelegant squawk from the thing trying to force dead sperm into her womb. A pitiful yelp that enticed her to look once more, even as she redoubled her efforts to sheer that prick in half and expel his invasion.

Rattling, the eyes behind the mask went

glassy. Pupils expanding to claim slow millimeters of watery blue, until the empty husk of rotting meat simply... melted away as if it never really were in the first place...

She blinked, squeezed her eyes tightly shut, and didn't stop until she could hear the rushing flood of effort pounding at her ear drums. "Not... not real," she mumbled, shivering with fever. A confusing blend of heated need keeping her skewered where she was. "Not real, not real, not—"

A distinctly male voice rumbled beneath her, groaning as rough fingers clutched at her hip with firm, yet tender fingers. "Feels real enough to me. Don't stop. So—*ugh*—fucking tight."

Her eyes snapped open and she met the lust-damp gaze of the male she had trapped between her knees...

Konjo. His eyes not the haunting, watery blue of a dead matron, but a stark mossy hazel. Throat undamaged, very much alive, and on the verge of spilling his seed for the second time.

Not a wound in sight.

17

Seething, Balkazar's chest vibrated with a near-constant growl. Outraged. Incensed beyond anything he'd ever known or felt, for he'd been *denied*. Unable to claim the privilege being Anhur afforded them, he and his Alpha had been made to watch the others breed their bitch. Dangling above the action. Helpless to intercede.

The net itself was outlandishly well-made. Tarred to seal the rope fibers, baked in the sun to make touching it an excruciating, prickly nightmare. Across his exposed skin, it had already left bright red lines of irritation. His palms were raw and bleeding, and no matter how hard he'd tried, Balkazar had been completely unable to break the sticky, criss-crossing ropes.

And then, just to wallow in the insult, the prince had lost his head and fucking marked him. An Anhur *Alpha*, lost to the rut with only a taste of the honey that lay between that girl's thighs.

Balkazar's nape throbbed, oozing where his Alpha had bitten him—though indeed, the war chief had returned the favor as best he could. Teeth stained with gore, he'd left his Alpha's throat and bicep dotted with the imprint of his incisors.

One brother turned against the other by a tiny slip of a girl.

A lowly Hathorian breeder completely swallowed up by her instincts, and she'd trapped them all without so much as bothering to gloat.

Choking on fury, Balkazar jerked when she cried out. Unable to look away from pale, flushed skin or the sinuous curve of her spine as it flexed and bowed. Breath hissing through clenched teeth, he exhaled a snarl when yet another orgasm was wrung from her slight body. An orgasm he was unable to feel wrapped snug around his cock, pulsing and teasing at his knot until it bloomed.

Despite his temper, the war chief was unable to blink. Attention riveted to the lewd scene below. Soaking his leathers with the steady drip of precome, he undulated in time with the rocking of her hips.

At his back, the twitch of the Alpha's cock pressing against his spine, damp where they'd been unable to turn away from each other no matter how hard they fought the netting.

"Sickle," he snapped, making the slender male flinch on the red rock below. "Get that fucking anchor cut."

"I'm"—Sickle took a gasping breath, fumbling the make-shift blade with shaking fingers—"I'm trying! Almost there..."

The crackle of snapping rope fibers serenaded his ears, Balkazar's every muscle going tense in preparation for the drop to the earth. To separate him from his Alpha before things became decidedly more... uncomfortable.

A scream teased at his senses, the high-pitched wail of a female who needed to take a knot and was being denied. Bred to be desperate for it.

For *him.*

Even if she didn't know it.

She cowered beneath the bulk of a male who outweighed her by easily six-fold, crying out with each desperate clash of pounding flesh. Eyes almost black, ears pressed flat, she squealed as Konjo worked that tight sheath with a knot that couldn't give her relief.

She surprised him, then. With one foot braced on slick, red rock, she huffed, arched, then flipped them both. Going so far as to wrap dainty fingers about Konjo's throat, dominating the massive hybrid as she tried to take what she needed. Her hips working in a furious blur as she rode another sticky load from the downed male.

Gasping, she scrambled free. Dripping. Shivering, a copious flood of cream gushed from her soiled channel, both male and female. None of it Anhur.

A fragile, tormented sound ripped free of her throat. A raw sound that made Balkazar's hackles rise where they were trapped against his Alpha's chest.

But instead of running, she stumbled to an unsteady stop a few feet away, swaying. Brow creased, she stood scratching at a spot on her jawline. Hugging her ribs and shivering.

Confused and still needy, the poor girl.

Desperate to sink his knot into that messy cunt, the war chief squirmed, setting the Alpha off when he snarled, "Sickle! *Now!*"

"It's almost—*there!*" the boy cried, leaping back as the rope snapped at last. Whistling as it whipped through the air.

Nothing happened.

No sudden drop, no breathtaking *thump...* or... at least not for the Anhur males.

Behind him, Keever and Micah crashed into the earth, howling and snapping at each other. Thrashing against the net's weight.

"Sickle, what the *fuck?*" the Alpha bellowed, trying to strain away from the wet spot spreading on Balkazar's hip. To reach the girl before the others left her a twitching ruin.

Keever got free first.

"Don't you *dare!*" Balkazar hissed at the new recruit, trying again to tear his way free until blood dripped to the ground below.

"Touch that bitch, and I will turn your marrow into soup, you ungrateful mongrel!"

For the first time since the hybrids had joined the pack, the war chief went ignored.

Sprinting flat out, Keever bellowed a challenge in the girl's face.

She managed to take a full step back before her knees went liquid. Before she melted and was caught, slung over a broad, dense shoulder, and spirited away.

"Sickle!" the Alpha bellowed, breath trembling on Balkazar's nape. Dominance shimmering in the air all around him. "Find that fucking anchor, or—"

"There's none left!" the boy cried, edging back from where Micah thrashed in the fallen net. "I cut both ropes already! And... and I can't see—I don't know where to look!"

Balkazar craned his neck back, tracing the inky black rope where it snaked through the foliage. It was there, in the sharp, zagging lines in the trees above. The fragmented mind of a female in the thrall of a natural season.

"Well, *that's* inconvenient," the war chief said, spotting their anchor at last—forty-five feet above unforgiving, rock-hard ground.

Following his gaze, Sickle paused, then said, "That clever minx," in a quiet, breathy tone under his breath. And then, "I'll climb for it, Balkazar. I'm sor—"

"No." Balkazar shifted, eyes flicking toward Keever's back. Watching as the Beta male sprinted toward the bubbling hot spring, then tossed the girl in. "It's a foolish risk." And one she was going to be punished for taking. Harshly. "Konjo!" he barked, and the freshly fucked hybrid flinched. Having the sense to look contrite, even as he struggled to tuck his thick, messy cock back into his leathers. "Get over here and boost Sickle up."

The Hathorian male shifted on the balls of his feet. Brow damp with anxious sweat. "Why?"

"Because—"

At the pool, the girl screamed then went silent. Keever scouring her fragile body of his pack brother's leavings, dunking her head under the water's surface in his haste.

An instant later, Micah was free of the netting. Muscles heaving, his hackles up. Dark eyes fixed to the spot where Keever had forced her to bend, sending a thick cock sluicing through delicate folds.

And Balkazar relaxed, grateful for the gentle, dark-skinned giant—no matter the urge to rut, Micah would not allow her to be harmed, much less drowned.

Despite the interruption and the demand throbbing in his pants, the war chief returned his eyes to Sickle. Dangerous and glittering— a solemn vow of retribution. "You're going to cut us free."

18

Breath leaked from her lips as she thrashed, bubbles tickled the fine hairs lining her cheeks. Her upper lip, forehead. Bodily submerged, she was scoured clean, thick fingers plumbing her depths. Purged of any trace of the other males who'd already been between her thighs.

Taking liberties where few were given.

But still, she was held beneath the surface until the bubbles began to slow. Until her chest fought and burned.

And when knuckles bumped her glands, deep inside, she gasped, sucking in half a lung full of heated water.

She came up spluttering, hissing with indignant rage—but the male at her back was too desperate to care. Not given a single moment to catch her breath, she was mounted. The head of a fat, blunt cock speared through tender flesh. Not bothering to tease, yet too big to batter his way in with only a single, vicious stroke, the hybrid had to fight for every last inch of conquered pussy.

"Wait—" she yelped, goosebumps rippling over her skin. Trying to scramble free of calloused, greedy fingers before she was drowned right there in the bubbling hot spring. Speared on a prick too big for her slight frame.

"Please—"

Stretching as he squeezed into that tight sheath, the hybrid at her back groaned. Deep and rough. A ragged huff against her nape, but that was all. Not a word of introduction. Not an ounce of civility.

He took her like a beast. Starved for female attention, he was unable to do anything but burrow.

Lips and nose dipping beneath the surface in his haste, she yielded the last inches of her slit to an unstoppable force. Blowing bubbles once more. Flailing with nothing to use for leverage, the pool too deep. Too wide to offer aid.

A hand found purchase in the floating locks of her hair. Made a fist between her ears, then pulled. Dragging her to the edge of the bathing pool by the roots of her hair, the animal at her back was forced to follow or be rejected.

She coughed up a grateful breath, making the cock lodged inside her kick and pulse.

Dark skin met her blurred vision, the bottom edge of flexing abs rippling too close. Her brain fogging with the scent of a heavy, masculine musk. All male, and yet...

Infertile.

She could smell it, just there. Hidden among the other many scents that told her who this male was.

A measure of confidence bloomed hot and twisty along her spine.

Hybrids, both of them. Unable to breed, they'd been born to fight but knew how to nurture. Twice the size of the Anhur, they were deadly and gentle.

And this was the first time she'd ever been able to really *look*.

Sparse, dense hair edged his nape, his shoulders, the top third of his spine—inherited from the sire—he appeared Anhur. But there was evidence of her kind in his broad, sloping features, too. She could see it in the point of his expressive, twitching ears. The slightly elongated canines.

A hybrid's knot may not be enough to milk her glands into submission... but two?

She smiled. Blinking water from her lashes.

Inviting them to give what she needed.

Uttering a soothing rumble, the hybrid before her returned her smile. Irises swallowed by the black inner ring, only the slimmest sliver of deep, earthy brown remained. He ignored the heavy, pulsing organ hanging between his legs and adjusted her with careful, firm nudges. His touch gentle— almost reverent as he draped her over the pool's edge.

She hissed as her nipples were dragged over rock, making the sensitive nubs stand stiff and alert. Making her clench around the thick shaft burning her insides.

Ebony skin rippled over bulging, scarred muscles. The only warning she got before the tip of a fat purple head smacked against her chin. Catching the corner of her mouth, her lips parting on a lewd sucking *pop*. Cock skipping over damp skin, leaving a tacky trail shining across her cheek.

Groaning at the back of his throat, he pulled back to meet her gaze, pushing the heavy curtain of wet, black hair off her forehead. Gathered it in fists at her nape.

And then, heedless of teeth or doing harm, that dark-skinned hybrid male pressed the tip of his prick to her tongue. He fed her a taste that made her gasp, connecting them with a string of pearly white.

Parted lips were an invitation too tempting to ignore, and—both hands fisted in her wet hair—he forced her jaws wider. Pushing until the lip of his helmet wedged between her teeth.

Another hand landed on the back of her skull, driving her forward until she gagged. Entire body flexing in one heave of desperate

rejection that went ignored. That was an-
swered by rumbling groans.

Impaled from end to end, the male at her
back lifted her from the water, took one step
forward, and left her to brace against the rippling muscle of the one leaking precome in
her mouth. A helpless position that saw her
pussy flush with slick once more. Easing the
friction water alone couldn't assuage.

A desperate snarl at her back, and she
was bumped up and over the edge of the
pool. Hips squashing the round globes of her
upturned bottom—forcing the other part of
the way down her throat.

Again, she gagged. Ribs heaving, sodden
sheath fluttering, she bore down. Choking.
Her *Biquea* glands cinched tight around that
shaft. Mercilessly forcing the breeding to
continue.

She was helpless. Spit roasted between
two hybrids—one trying to force a thick cock
down her throat, the other doing his
damnedest to help see that desire bear fruit
as he pounded into her from behind.

Truly fucking now, the slap of hips sent
water to shower over them all, the warm current teasing and kissing her clit with every
frenetic lurch of engorged flesh.

"Hnnnghh," she grunted, tears prickling
at the backs of her eyes. Each thrust saw that
dark prick shoved down her gullet just a little
deeper. Each snapping twitch of hybrid hips
bumped her closer to milking the cock

spearing into her sodden heat with a blissful release of her own.

Even the fingers leaving marks on her hips served only to wind her tighter—a gift from her first natural season. It crossed the lines hardwired in her brain. Told her body she wasn't enduring life-threatening treatment, but getting exactly what she needed. Sending blood and hormones to prepare her to take more abuse than any but an experienced Hathorian breeder could endure.

She was meant to go for days like this—trained for it. Days where she ate and drank nothing but what her master pumped down her throat. Where the need for sleep was replaced with nothing but the need to breed.

And she knew, even in the heat of this madness...

... This was only the beginning.

Winding both hands through hair darker than his skin, an impressive girth stretched her jaws wide as they could go. Using her throat as he might abuse his fist, he worked toward an orgasm. Sweat and water trickling over the ridges of a defined abdomen.

She swallowed the head leaking sweet, salty fluid, feeling the muscles of her throat work and bump over that sensitive glans. Feeling her walls flood with slick as a challenging roar issued above her, then behind.

A warning.

Neither would last, both competing to be the first to seed her, and she wasn't ready.

Fingers tightened on her hips, her scalp. The pace between her thighs grew frantic. Uneven. Enough that she could feel it when his balls began to boil, shaft bloating and thick.

In her mouth, a cock thickening down her throat. Her lips stretched until they were an obscene white ring.

Bliss.

Hormones flooded her system. Replacing terror with lust. Pain with ecstasy. Drooling from front and back, unable to worry her poor, neglected clitoris, she could only brace between them.

And hope.

Rumbling against her forehead, one long, scarred forearm extended back. Traced her back from shoulder to the ridged scar where her tail had once been, the dark male toyed with her puckered asshole. Ringing that tight muscle for a moment before he sank lower. Before he slipped his index into her pussy, no matter the girth stretching her out.

Out of sight, covering her back, a possessive snarl issued challenge. The savage snap of hips that served only to illuminate what was happening inside her. That a thick finger knuckled another male's shaft, invasive and lacking all sense of propriety.

It sent a taboo thrill zinging through her nerves. Pushed her just a little closer—

The finger disappeared, the cock down

her throat withdrawing as that finger was sucked deep and licked clean.

Gasping, the girl shivered, tongue darting out to taste. Her gaze searching the deep, brown eyes glaring down at her.

It was a respite. Only the space of a single, ragged breath before he was sluicing through her lips and down her throat once more. Before his thick finger returned to her abused quim and plunged in alongside a leaking prick.

But this time, the dark male didn't taste it—no, he pulled back just a little and pressed into her asshole. Filling her holes, all three at once.

It was too much for some.

With a final, shuddering roar, an explosion erupted within her.

Fingers bruising, knot expanding, she was filled. Rope after rope of thick cream sprayed into shivering cunt, bathing her thirsty, fussy cervix with seed that couldn't flourish.

But she didn't care.

No, there was nothing but the gracious fingers that *finally* sought to work at her clit. Flicking the overwrought little bean back and forth until she gushed milky Hathorian fluids.

She came with force enough to evict the male still pulsing inside her passage. Teeth threatening to click shut around the slab of meat plumbing her windpipe, the other was unable to stop his semen from slithering from her depths with an obscene *plop*. Dripping into the swirling warm water. And with a final, satisfied sigh, a great weight collapsed over her back. A chin on her shoulder. Breath teasing her cheek, he fumbled between them. Sinking back into her tight passage until his knot was caught by her glands.

It wasn't over.

With a grunt of his own, the male down her throat picked up the pace. Heedless of slapping palms or the desperate sounds she made, he fucked her throat with wild abandon, black eyes unable to tear away from her upturned face. One fist clenched in her hair, tugging at the roots for leverage. Her left ear caught in a tight fist.

And then, withdrawing his forefinger from her asshole, he wrapped that same hand around her airway. Using her throat to jerk himself off, drool was smeared around her lips before his fist returned to anchor in her hair.

He was close, she could feel it in the way he further expanded her jaws. In the erratic snapping pulse of his hips flexing and working toward a glorious finish.

Stars glittered at the edge of her vision. Closing in. Her head spinning and bouncing.

And yet, the treatment wasn't new to her. Nor to any of the females imprisoned in the harem.

Hadim had favored rough oral—all the girls knew how to quicken his release. A secret passed from matron to Omega, for all knew of the whispers of what happened if their master was allowed to plunder without restraint.

Of the girls who went and never returned.

The male rutting down her throat was *nothing* compared to the brand of cruelty she'd been born to endure.

All he needed was a little... push...

Balanced on her left palm with the dead weight of a massive hybrid slung across her back, she slipped one dainty, wet hand between glistening, sable thighs. Giving exactly as good as she got, she reached further than the bulge of a heavy sack, past flexing cheeks, and found her mark.

The edges of a smile puckered her stretched lips.

A ring of muscle was tested. Breached. Stretched until her second knuckle was buried and wriggling.

Her reward?

A face full of pubes and twitching, kicking cock spurting salty seed into her gut.

She coughed and took him deeper by accident. Coughed again and jerked her finger out of his clenching ass, then slapped at his thigh. Silently demanding he ease off, let her breathe.

Obedient hybrid male that he was, he withdrew. Coating her tongue with rope after rope of sperm until it spilled over her glistening lips.

"Keever," he said, pointing to the unconscious male draped over her back. "Micah," he added, touching his own chest. The tip of his finger going pale as he pressed it into a thatch of curled chest hair, making the skin dimple.

A considerate gentleman.

19

Micah gasped. Still twitching and dripping, the little breeder perched before him—half in, half out of the hot spring. Lips stained with seed, Keever's weight slung across her back.

With a shaking breath, Micah maneuvered the pair so he might uncouple them. Pulling Keever's long, slender knot from soiled walls with a *pop* that preceded the hot gush of sperm.

The girl didn't so much as flinch, her pupils completely blown. Inky black gaze traced his nudity, enthralled by a powerful natural season. Desperate to continue being bred until she was ripe and gravid.

His cock twitched with renewed vigor, for though he'd reached orgasm, Micah's knot had gone unstimulated. The compulsion to breed left unfulfilled, no matter that it was false to begin with. An inherited whisper, a constant reminder that hybrids had no bloodline.

No legacy.

Hathorian eyes flicked to his prick, her black hair floating in a cloud where it wasn't hanging in lanky strands across her face. "Please," she whispered, lips quivering where they sat, just above the surface of the water.

She'd never be round with his kits, but by the Nine in their fiery kingdom, Micah could *pretend*, couldn't he? Just for a few moments, or until the Anhur males finally managed to fight their way free. Before he received the beating he'd earned for taking liberties with their property.

Micah tore his gaze from that inky stare, brushed away reaching fingers, and hauled Keever off her back. Depositing him on the hard red stone, so the fool wouldn't drown in his post-orgasmic haze.

At his back, the Anhur had gone eerily silent where they hung in their net. Watching as he reached for the girl next. As he twisted a length of black silk about his fist and dragged her over the stone by the root of her hair.

Hair fine as silk that clung to his fingers.

She mewled, limbs twitching as if she meant to struggle but hadn't the strength or will.

"Micah!" his Alpha hissed, voice pitched low and laced with command. A warning.

And for the first time since joining their company, Micah ignored his duty.

Bluntly defiant, his hackles rose up about his shoulders, lower back flexing where the ghost of his tail stood tall and proud. Micah embraced the instinct he could consummate but never bring to fruition and took a female for his own.

An eager female who squirmed toward instead of away.

Nudging at her opening with the blunt tip of his cock, Micah set his prize on a ledge of red stone. Smiled when she trilled, licking herself clean. Searching for any lost droplets of his thick cream.

"Hurry the fuck up, Sickle," the Alpha snarled, and the little Hathorian female growled at the Anhur males suspended in nets. Bared dainty, blunted teeth while her chest rumbled with a pretty snarl.

Issuing threats, despite her diminutive size and submissive gender.

And though his heart sang with pride for the fierce little thing helpless to fight her own body, not even a hybrid could resist such a challenge from a lowly Hathorian.

An *Omega.*

No, he grew desperate to see her humbled and tamed, mewling for his come.

There was the ring of something deeper there, something more than merely reacting to instinct. At least for him. For where she'd been born of selective lineages to produce litters of healthy, *big* hybrids, he'd been bred for war.

Born to die.

Trained in the fighting sands before he'd learned to walk, Micah sat on the ledge and set the slight female astride his thighs. One eye on the pert, bruised nipples shivering a scant few inches from his lips. The other monitoring Sickle's progress as he struggled to free the Anhur. Refusing to give up his back, even for this.

Micah caught one rosy peak between his teeth. Gnawing the tight bead as Sickle sawed at the ropes, only halfway through.

There was time enough to indulge, and he did so with a vengeance. Cradling narrow, incredible hips meant to nourish life, Micah dwarfed her. Could crush her bones on a whim, yet took great care. Spread pale thighs wide, obscene and lewd, watching her drip what Keever had lodged deep inside.

He marveled at the contrast between their skin, at the deep, rich color of his knob as it smeared through a pink mess. As he teased and mashed her clit, working over the seam where she went together before parting glossy folds of flesh.

Tight didn't begin to describe the silken grip of her cunt. The pain of impaling her beyond engorged *Biequa* glands—the most inflamed he'd ever seen, much less felt.

Still, he didn't stop.

She begged him not to with the slant of her eye. The desperate, gasping part of slack lips. The way she locked around his girth and forced him to stay until she was stuffed full as he could make her. Until his knob bumped the face of that final gate.

Her cervix.

Where he could worship but never desecrate.

Mocking him for being born to her kind, but sired by another.

A hybrid.

He snarled and pressed deeper still. Making his prick bend deep within her soiled channel, he lifted her. Spreading a female already milky with another's salty stains, she left a ring of progress around his ebon dick. Slowly forcing her to take more of what he had with each demanding press. Every fist full of flesh and muscle, kneading the globes of her tight ass. Forcing her down.

He reached around, fingers smearing slick and clotted cream down the length of his shaft, because Micah knew what was coming for the wild little female. Knew, even having only just met her, that he'd protect her as fiercely as he protected his new pack.

That he'd protect her *from* his pack mates, if it came to it.

And so it was that he gathered a dollop of her cream mixed with Keever's. Guiding her until she regained functional control over her limbs and began to ride him, he sucked one of her nipples between his lips and pinched with sharp teeth that had never been filed short. Distracting her as he poked at the crinkled bud nestled between milky cheeks. Spreading that pearly dollop over her asshole before pressing in, just as she'd done to him.

That singular feeling—of his finger wriggling through the wall separating her cunt from her bowel—almost undid him. Nearly shamed him with a premature spilling as the image of her stuffed with two cocks popped into his slick-addled brain.

He could feel her glands just there, hard as stone. Hot and ripe.

But that very thought saw him slow and press a second finger into her bottom. Trying to milk her glands from both sides of her channel, even as he stretched her out. Readying her for the Anhur driven utterly beyond reason by her scent. By her devious nature, and the very hands that clung to him now.

He couldn't stop them from taking what they needed from the Hathorian female, nor did he want to see them go without. The Anhur deserved to feel the glorious silken grip milking him dry, just as much as he did.

Maybe more.

But Micah would see her go undamaged, if only so he could take her again when they woke in the morning. And again the next day following. And again and again and *again*, until he'd made up for the decades of going without.

So he pressed a third finger into her ass,

preparing her second hole for the coming assault.

To be used.

The female shivered, bracing on his chest with delicate spread fingers. Fucking back against his prick and thick, invading digits in her ass, she groaned. Smashing his knob against her limit. Overstimulating the massive warrior more than happy to be used, even as he prepared her to be mounted. Front and back.

"Come for me, Omega," Micah gasped, sweat beading across his dark brow. "Take what you need."

Face framed by a halo of midnight locks, she rode him. Pawed at the space between shoulder and jaw and rode him.

Fingers spearing through her distended rosebud, Micah drove her to higher speeds. Used his leverage in her ass to propel her toward his base and away. Making sure to grind her engorged bean against the early bloom of his knot, just to hear her yelp. Just to watch her obsidian eyes roll back and feel her tighten, her glands pulsing against the tips of questing fingers. Crushing his knot—demanding compliance.

When his knot began to bloat in earnest, he snarled, slapped one massive palm down on her flexing cheek, and sent her spiraling into bliss. Riding a wave of gentle pain mixed with pleasure, she shook above him.

"That's a good girl," he rasped and

suckled at her nipple once more. As if she were swollen with milk and heavy with his young. "That's it—*ughhh*—take it all, Omega!"

Shuddering, Micah unleashed his second load. This one bouncing off the roof of her cunt, spilling out around his pulsing member and weak knot.

The fantasy shattered as his cream spilled over. His knot as wide as he'd ever felt it, and still, it wasn't enough to seal in his useless semen.

But he settled back with a smile. Heart thudding against his ribs, a tight Hathorian sheath sucking the life from his balls in rhythmic, clenching pulls.

Content.

20

Heart thudding, her pulse throbbed at the base of her throat. Her temples. In the slippery channel milking a weak knot. Her glands clenching in the aftershocks of orgasm that wasn't nearly enough.

Already she was beginning to ache, the little ball of heat winding tighter and tighter. Ripe with tension that demanded *more*.

"Again," she rasped, fingers spread across hard slabs of muscle. Nails bumping over old, raised scars.

Micah shook his head, throat clicking around a swallow. "'M sorry, Omega," he said, not unkindly. Deep voice rumbling straight through his prick into her depths. "Can't."

Her ears flicked back, blunt teeth flashing.

"Hybrids don't rut." He palmed the pale globes of her ass, flexing to drive his softening prick deeper. "Not really. Need more time to recover than an Anhur."

A furious snarl echoed at her back, the Alpha howling his rage at being made to watch.

Hadim.

Clarity returned to her then, as she sat with palms braced against Micah's chest. Flushed with orgasm, panting and out of breath, she was splayed across his thick thighs and stretched obscenely wide around a fat cock that had no business fitting inside her.

Not while her master watched, death glittering in his one good eye.

Oblivious, Micah sighed as his pole slithered from her depths with a wet sucking hiss. Rejected by swollen glands, it bowed under its own weight. Not quite limp, globs of pearly white sperm burping from the void left in that tight, inflamed sheath. The tip a healthy rose-pink angled toward the red rock. His shaft an earthy-brown so rich it made no secret of how deep that beast had been in her cunt—a ring of frothy white marked Micah's progress.

"Go on," the hybrid rumbled, nudging her thighs. "Go to them. The Anhur will give you what you need, pet. What I... can't. An' you're in luck." He spread her labia with the pads of dark thumbs, staring at the stretched lips frosted in white. "Our Alpha is a Karahmet prince. Had a harem an' everything. He'll be good to you for your first heat."

"No," she spat, teeth flashing and staggered from Micah's lap. Slipping on the slick, red stone, her ears pressed flat to her skull. Limbs trembling with helpless need, with the effort to refuse an Anhur male making unspoken demands.

But refuse she did.

Giving them her back, the girl turned to the hot springs. Away from Hadim and the retribution she knew would come. The claws and bruises. Slicing into her flesh, he would leave her marked if he bothered to leave her alive...

She stumbled when she stepped in a puddle of fluids, then went to her knees with a thump, a pained cry. Both hands braced wide, elbows locked. Her pelvis pulsing with need none but Hadim had ever been able to ease.

Having exhausted all of her other playthings, she squealed a wordless protest.

She needed, but refused to submit.

Hot, throbbing agony oozed through her veins. Her skin. The base of her spine, where her tail tried to flex in a graceful, alluring arch of invitation none could see.

Rounded ass swaying to and fro, keening high at the back of an abused throat, she began to crawl. Hips tipping up, she presented even as she set flimsy claws into stone and worked toward a freedom she'd never have again. Displaying swollen lips and a splash of seed that clung to slick flesh.

She saw Micah stand, the depleted hybrid

retreating after he'd taken his fill. The heavy weight of his dick now shrunken and soft, he made way for the Anhur to take his place.

Abandoning her where she lay.

Whining, she dragged her knees over the stone. Breath hitching, a fragile sob escaped swollen lips. "*Nnnest,*" she whispered, rattling over the lonely syllable. Seeking the comfort of instinct, when there was none to be had elsewhere. Her ears drooping as her strength began to wane, as adrenaline gave way to scorching heat. Liquid desire. "Just need... my... my..."

Shouted cries of triumph shattered the glassy haze enveloping her mind. And she looked, knowing she shouldn't. That doing so might well be her last free decision.

But she couldn't help it.

And it was too late to run... to get to her spear. To hide.

Hadim was nearly free.

21

"I can't go any further," Sickle gasped, sweating as he worked with arms raised high above his head. Sawing at the tar-coated ropes keeping the Anhur stranded and out of the competition. "I—I can't reach."

Sneering, the Alpha shoved his hand through the net, palm up. Reaching. "Give it to me," he said, fingers clicking until the rough handle of Sickle's make-shift blade landed with a slap. Jagged edges threatening to tear skin, until he set it to the itchy ropes. "Move," he snapped, shoulders bunching as he worked. Trying to saw at the cords beneath his ass, no matter that doing so made him rock against Balkazar.

Made him throb and drip.

The Omega mewled, pained and desperate. Her *Biquea* glands swollen to the point of acute agony the likes of which he'd never witnessed before, visible from even this distance.

This was no lowly runaway on the cusp of maturity, fleeing the change that would see males fight over breeding rights—females like *that* were easily serviced by a hybrid's weak knot. It was a handy trick, to use a well-trained hybrid to subdue females in heat. To keep their wares pristine, their wombs untouched and hovering at peak-value. Break them in without hardening them off.

But not this girl.

Micah's girth should have been enough to at least partially relieve her—and yet, she was as agitated as any he'd ever seen.

Which could only mean…

Wonder lit the Alpha's face for an instant. A brief moment of realization and stark hunger for a thing he'd thought lost to him forever.

This girl was an escaped harem slave.

Somehow, by the grace of the Nine, she was here. Thriving in the beyond.

There would be no lengthy training period, no messy tears of a virgin needing to be broken in.

She'd been bred for endurance, schooled in the arts of giving pleasure, her bloodline was ancient—one he recognized, if he couldn't quite place it. Hand-chosen with the highest pedigree, her *Biquea* glands had grown hard, resistant to abuse from anything but a truly massive knot of a dominant Anhur male.

Maybe even a prince.

The thought saw his hackles rise with scarcely restrained glee.

It was how the ruling Anhur preferred their breeding Hathorians—desperate to be knotted, tolerant to lengthy periods of neglect, and utterly ignorant of their own bodies. Oblivious of their history or what they were built to endure.

He squinted at her face, searching for recognition beneath the hanks of sopping hair. The flushed cheeks.

Instead, his one-eyed gaze was drawn to the bruised globes of a tight female ass, at the scar where her tail had once been and where Micah couldn't keep her full. Where she leaked and gushed and went unsatisfied around a knot that hadn't a chance of subduing her.

Only he could give her what she truly needed. What he'd given countless others just like her.

Relief.

Enough compression on her inflamed glands to milk them until they were empty. To release the built-up chemicals that would trigger her eggs to drop and allow him to seed the wily little bitch.

He'd been denied long enough. Forced to watch as she'd been pumped full, the Alpha bellowed. Shredding the ropes and his palms, both.

The netting snapped beneath the makeshift blade, exposing the hanging

Anhur to a void. A sharp drop and a dull thud.

Gasping, the Alpha was up first, fighting free of the net, he landed a few savage strikes to the back of Balkazar's skull. Not stopping until the war chief was limp. Giving himself the advantage, he left Balkazar laying in the netting. Out cold, yet still twitching toward the female.

Frozen where she'd stopped, she watched his approach with wide, dark eyes.

And despite the urge to rush toward her, he slowed. Enthralled.

There was challenge in her glare, even now. A note of defiance, no matter that she hadn't a hope of escaping.

Not now.

Not ever.

A dainty pink tongue darted out, wetting. Tasting. Lingering on the bow of her lower lip, even as she made to scramble back.

Rumbling deep in his chest, the Alpha's hand went to his pant front. The laces torn in haste.

He'd watched her take the lesser males, one by one. He'd watched as she allowed each of them to spill within her and knot. He'd watched Micah pour sperm down her throat and send her deeper into the haze *he* wanted to inspire.

And yet, she refused him? Deliberately ignored his orders. His commands to be set free so he could ease her pain.

He'd never known an Omega to deny her caste. To fight what she'd been born to do—and while in the thrall of a natural season, no less.

It was a wonder.

A rarity.

Refusing to submit could only mean the little bitch *wanted* to be conquered. That she was testing him to see if he were worthy of filling her womb. Of claiming her as he might a natural queen.

Forever.

Commanding without words, the Alpha snarled. Hackles rising and on full display, his chest rumbled with a deep compulsion to obey. Taking his time in the approach instead of succumbing to the instinct to throw her down in the dirt and fuck her pregnant.

"Please," she whispered, cringing back from a display that should have seen her melt and submit. Oh, she presented her back, all right. But it wasn't to be mounted—the little bitch began to crawl in the opposite direction.

Nostrils flared, the Alpha kicked at her ankles just to watch her gape. "Enough of this, Omega," he spat, words bumping over the edges of his furious snarl. "You can't escape. There's nowhere you can go that I won't find you now."

She twisted, terror etched into pale Hathorian features.

"Oh, yes," he breathed and pumped his fist over his length. "You're mine."

A strained sound splintered through her lips. Great, fat tears spilling over dark lashes.

"Beg for it," he said, looming above her. Stroking his cock as she shuddered and went still. "Beg me to stuff you full of this knot, little slut."

A drop of drool spilled over her lips, ebon eyes rolling in her skull as her glands flexed around nothing. Forcing her to stop, head hanging low. Sweat glistening on her low back, her nape. Dripping from the tips of reddened, inflamed nipples.

The Alpha smiled, cruel and ravenous. "Look at you," he rattled, pressing his every available advantage. "Desperate for this knot. Don't worry, Omega. I'm going to mount you." He knelt behind her, taking his cock by the root. "You're going to take my seed deep as you can," he cooed, slapping his palm down on her left cheek. Squeezing a handful of ripe flesh, he pulled her petals apart even when they clung and stuck. "And then," he said, sweeping his prick through the mess of slick and come, "you're going to milk my knot for more."

Burbling, she pushed back. Tried to take his helm inside to ease the ache, even as she whispered, "Nooo."

"Oh, *yesss*," he replied, balls aching. Pulsing with every frantic flutter of his heart. It was a primal demand to seat himself deep as he could go in her spoiled walls and rut until his muscles gave out. Until he erased the other males paltry attempts to take what was his. An instinct screaming for him to force his sperm through the barrier guarding her womb, just so he could watch her belly grow round with his young.

A litter of hybrid kits to grow his army.

But this runaway harem slave needed more than a simple breeding. She wouldn't tumble into desperate, blind love around his knot like an untried virgin. The state of her *Biquea* glands told him there'd be no manipulating her with hormones, for he knew better than most what it took to turn a Hathorian female into a prince's breeder.

The sheer amount of abuse and neglect.

A female like this wouldn't know to be grateful for a gentle approach—she'd condemn it.

No, what this defiant creature needed was a *new* master.

The Alpha wrapped his hand in her thick, black locks and wrenched her head back. Sending her into a submissive state with little more than a flick of his wrist.

"I'm going to breed you, Omega," he whispered, lips tracing her ear. The slur slipping off his tongue with cruel ease, his prick weeping pearly tears of eager joy. "You're going to spend the rest of your life producing soldiers for my army."

A ragged sob burst from her lips. Wet with spittle, edged with helpless desperation. "P-please, Ha—"

But he was the one who needed, so he clapped a palm over her mound. Right hand snaking around her hips and between her legs, he plugged her weeping cunt with his three thickest fingers. Spread her labia and traced her opening. He worked her, then, playing in the mess his brothers had left, teasing her glands as she cried and lurched.

She moaned, gushing over his fingers. Surrendering her weight, her breath whistling and cold against his palm.

Sensing victory, he grinned. Eager to sink into the wet heat between her thighs at last, he shoved her back to hands and knees. Positioning her so that he might see where her tail had been, the elegant, twisting ink that traced her spine and marked her lineage. All so he could run the blunt edge of his nails over the scar and watch her come undone.

In an instant, pretty mewling became guttural. Shivering muscles began to spasm, and the few words she had left devolved into an untethered wail of denial.

But the Alpha wasn't finished. Had scarcely even begun.

He dipped his cock into her heated channel, groaning when she began to clamp down. Compressing his knob in a silken fist.

"Such a tight cunt, Omega," he crooned, mocking as he made another fist in tangled, wet hair as he began to burrow deeper. Fighting her *Biquea* glands for every millimeter gained. "And here I thought Micah had ruined you for all of us."

She hiccupped, but said nothing more.

Kneading her hips, twisting her neck to keep her helpless beneath him, the Alpha sank inside. Enjoying every stolen inch. The press of glands swollen to ludicrous proportions gave her the grip of an innocent—gushing slick and come, the welcoming passage of a seasoned whore.

"Ugh," he spat and slapped her ass to make her clench around him. "Perfect little breeder. Take it."

But before he sank his knot where she needed it, he withdrew. Sluicing through the tight ring just inside, he teased her to the edge of madness. Worked her clenching channel until he'd purged her depths of any hint of another male, the mushroom-flare of his cock scraping her clean until her glands expressed a rush of fresh slick.

"Mmmphh," she grunted, cheeks red. Eyes black and rimmed in white. "Pllluhh—"

That was all it took to make the breeder come. To make her to spray his thighs with milky fluid too thin to be mistaken for semen.

She only sobbed harder, thrashing as he tormented her with the tapered edge of his knot. Rubbing at the front wall of her cunt, he withheld the shuddering impact of hips on flesh. Reveling in the thrill of debasing the feisty thing as she whined beneath him.

"Beg," he said again, pinning her with left

hand, wrenching her head back with the right. "Beg for this knot or suffer without it. I get to come either way."

Instead of obeying his command, a midnight black glare rolled to meet his working eye. And she scowled, showing the smooth line of blunted teeth.

When she snarled defiance, the Alpha fell in love.

And then she stopped him cold in the middle of a promising rut.

"Hadim, *please!*"

22

A shadow moved through the forest. Silent, yet watched by the small woodland creatures who knew to be wary of an apex predator. Who knew that to stalk the hunter was to grow fat on the easy bounty of discarded scraps.

Without breaking so much as a twig, the hunter oozed from the shadows that clung and begged for his return. A shaft of sunlight brightened hair matted with mud and filth, highlighting a mane that hung in clumps from bare shoulders. Dusty skin coated in a protective layer of grime—camouflage from hungry, opportunistic lurkers.

And through the gloom, eyes that gleamed with a rich amber hue. Unnatural.

The most obvious sign of one plagued with the Trax virus.

Infected.

Thick shoulders bunched as the hunter

paused, braced against a tree. Gaze fixed to a small herd of four-legged grazers.

Deadly, razor sharp antlers curved back from a muscular torso—proficient in disemboweling a predator without much effort, the antlers also served to shield the back of the neck. The creature's only true vulnerability, evolved to be inaccessible from vicious predators more lethal than even he.

There were no weapons clutched in those massive, calloused hands. Nothing to throw, no traps to set. There was only him and the weapon his body had become.

The hunter lifted one heavy foot, paused, then placed it between leaf litter and exposed stone. Pressing ever closer to the herd. Senses keyed to the slightest change in their mood. In the environment around him, and most of all, in the way his bulk moved through the wood. Taking care to remain hidden until the herd forgot to be wary, when they relaxed into the beautiful warm day and ignored the impulse to run from ravenous shadows.

Opportunity came when the herd's bull dipped his heavy head to graze. His guard down, swiveling ears and deadly horns relaxed as he munched on sweet summer grass. Surveying his females with a lazy flick of a short, bushy tail.

The hunter edged closer, mane rising up where it could, where the clumps of dirt and matting allowed for such a display that would go unseen by any who could comprehend the warning.

And there he would wait, muscles locked. Lurking in the shadows for the perfect moment to strike.

It came when the bull bounded off in chase of a female displaying the signs of fertility. She dropped to the detritus, her slender twisting horns leaving deep gouges in the forest floor where she dragged them through the dirt. The ridge of fur along her back tightened and stood stiff, musk glands exposed to the humid afternoon air. Signaling her readiness.

Abandoning his herd in the heat of the moment, the bull went wild. Snorting and puffing, a pink cock slid from furry sheath. Twisted and thrashed against the female's rump.

When the bull mounted up, the hunter struck.

In an explosion of pent-up energy, he lunged from his perch. Claws fully extended, a bellowing roar was expelled from the bottom of his gut—one that made the herd flinch as one being, a hive-mind of terrified flesh moving in the same instinctive direction.

Away.

But the hunter already had his prize by the throat.

A sickly yearling with hardly enough bulk to last through the winter. Horns not yet fully grown and not the deadly weapon the bull would use to defend his herd. This young buck had a bent foreleg, where it may have broken and healed. Knit back together wrong.

It was a swift death, if bloody. A simple flex of deadly claws that burrowed through fur and skin, tore through arteries, and cut off blood supply to the brain before the spinal column was severed. Efficient. Neat. Easy.

Chest rumbling with a contented purr, the hunter slung the young beast over his shoulder. Making a sling of forelegs and belly, careful of the horns just beginning to poke through their yearling felt. The razor-sharp edges encased in fuzz.

And with his burden secured, he began the trek through dense brush. Retracing his original path with full, confident strides. No longer stalking on the edge of shadows, but stealthy all the same. At ease in the wood, where few could challenge his dominance.

The hunter stopped at a small creek, dumped the grazer in a heap of stiffening limbs, then stretched his back until it popped. Hands on hips, crimson stains streaking across the contours of his back. Pooled in the dips and tracing the valleys, the blood had already drained away.

Fertilizer for the wild things that followed in his wake.

He made quick work of the carcass—in minutes, the abdomen was unzipped, choice organs separated from scrap, skin hauled from meat in three experienced tugs, scraped clean of the remaining pulp, and set to dry in the heat of the afternoon sun. Finally, when everything else had been done, a hook was run through the ankle tendons. An anchor set downstream, he tossed the meat into the narrow creek to wash away the last of the fluids.

He'd be long gone before any carrion eaters found their way to the scent of a fresh kill.

Stomach rumbling, the hunter claimed a jiggly slab of liver. Balanced on his haunches, he mashed the tender offal between his back molars. And no matter the acidic tingle of raw organ meat, it was creamy and rich. The earthy flavor of wild game still clinging to the memory of iron and the purpose it once served.

The rush of nutrients and vitamins made his head spin, his throat stick around a tacky swallow. And with a low groan, he stood, ambling toward the river. Pausing only to taste the wind, searching for danger that lurked beyond mere sight.

There was nothing but silence. The gentle breeze and the whisper of water bubbling over stone.

Kneeling, he dipped one massive hand into the creek, drawing up a palm full of sweet, crisp liquid.

All it took was a sip.

One wonderful, impossible sip and he knew.

Slick. In the water.

And not just slick, but a perfect match. He could taste it at the back of his skull. It lit up his brain with a barb of stark realization, of instant unwavering belief and dedication to a new path. A pulse of liquid heat shot through his nervous system, making his cock swell and bloat.

Bewildered, he turned wide, amber eyes upriver. Nostrils flared, head tipped back, he searched for any hint of that precious fluid on the breeze—and found none.

But the hunter needed no convincing. His body had hardened, pupils swallowing the sinister ring of color as his mane grew rigid.

The rut.

It struck hard. Fast. Descending with an unnatural weight that consumed everything, leaving behind only hunger. Possessive, ravenous starvation for the breeder producing that particular blend of scents and flavors.

His.

Cock weeping and painfully hard, his balls drew tight against his body. Giving greater access to a blend of deadly hormones not yet seen before, for the hunter had been infected with Trax for *years*. Mutated on a genetic level to endure the price of living so long with the deadly virus, he was changed. No longer Anhur, but something else. Bigger and faster.

Utterly feral.

Fixated upriver, he coughed up a snarl. Teeth snapping shut, lips peeled back. And then, as his testicles continued to dump white-hot fury into his veins, a guttural, bellowing roar erupted from deep in his belly. A primal challenge to anything with ears and a cock that a dominant male was staking claim on *that* pussy. Declaring ownership of the slick gushing from the cunt he would reshape to suit his monstrous knot.

Willing to kill any who might take what was his, he would lay their bodies at her feet. Broken into pieces and strung through the trees. Their screams a serenade, their innards a beautiful, gory mosaic of his devotion to the female that would whelp his young.

Vibrating with eager rage, the hunter crashed into the wood. Ignoring the shadows that begged him to melt into their embrace, he was a blur darting between the trees. A juggernaut on a mission.

In his wake, only a skinless carcass.

Prepared and forgotten.

23

"Hadim, *please!*" she gasped, begging just as he'd commanded her to do—her voice going soft and ragged around *the wrong name.* One that shocked him sober, for there wasn't a male alive who the Alpha despised more.

That they looked so much alike was a curse he'd long grown weary of carrying.

To be reminded of it now, in this precious moment of victory, served only to ignite his temper. Pouring lye in open, infected wounds that refused to mend.

But there was something else.

Something that soothed his fury with a far more satisfying reward. A revelation.

There was but *one* way she could have known that insufferable prick. But a single reason she would mistake *him* for Hadim—this miraculous, escaped Hathorian female had once belonged to the named Heir of the Karahmet throne. Hadim himself.

Trained to know only what Hadim had bothered to teach her. Wholly ignorant of her heritage, her biology, or the workings of her hormonal cycle that had ensnared her so fully, she was a creature of unfathomable value.

That she was here at all was a miracle, until he realized how much she must have gone through to simply survive. And then he knew it to be *impossible* that she was standing before him at all. In heat. Defiant. Healthy and absent any hint of the Trax virus.

But to know she was *Hadim's*? That she'd escaped her harem, navigated through the city, and had evaded the packs of roving, desperate males starving for a taste of female flesh. Managed to get through the wall and survived the wilds only to succumb to her nature at his feet?

His cock pulsed, a band of hot steel flexing against her swollen walls.

She was a divine gift. A clear sign that he still held favor with the Nine in their fiery hall.

She was his to do with as he pleased. Soiled beyond cleaning. *Ruined* by Hadim... just as he had been.

To know that she might have contributed to his fall, to the scars mangling the right side of his face. The eye that had been popped beneath Hadim's claws and now saw only the faintest shimmer of light? It was her fault, at least in part, for the hybrids who'd made his own army kneel had marched straight from *this* pussy.

One of her hybrid sons had slaughtered some of his.

A growl rumbled up, racing bile to be the first of the vitriol that spilled from his lips.

"I hate you," she whispered, making him pause. Coiled to strike. "I've spent these last moons praying for your death. Begging the Nine to give me justice for the horrors you've committed. Just kill me," she breathed, inky black gaze liquid as she glared, tears threatening to spill with a blink. "You might have my body. My womb. But I will *never* let your spawn live. They will never draw a single breath."

And for a moment, as he stared down into the abyss of hatred and spite, the Alpha knew a moment of camaraderie he'd never had with a female. An Omega. That she had suffered abuse at Hadim's hand wasn't obvious, so much as it was expected.

But to see her stand against her demon, misplaced as her anger might be, gave him pause of another sort altogether. The edges of an idea began to form in the haze of a stalled rut.

Vengeance.

He could take it from *her*.

All the wrongs Hadim had left staining his skin, his ruined face, blinded right eye, the loss of his hybrid sons and the harem who'd whelped them... All of it.

"Do you like my scars," he snarled, knowing she saw her master, he pressed closer to her upturned face. Forcing her to see only the damage Hadim had wrought and not the tiny differences between them. "I got them just for you, Omega."

Her ears flicked back, the scent of terror stinging the back of his sinuses. Blunted teeth flashed white in the gloom, but she said nothing. Didn't so much as try to pull away.

"Look at you," he cooed, touching her swollen lower lip with the pad of his finger. His grin spreading, for he knew exactly how to play the part of her master. Careful not to add specifics, he said, "You're desperate for this knot, hmm? I shouldn't have bothered to hunt you down." He sneered, catching one bruised nipple between forefinger and thumb. "Should have known all I needed to do was wait, and you'd come to me. Desperate for this knot."

At this, she recoiled, nipple popping free. She stumbled, slipping in a puddle of viscous fluids. On her face, the battle between terror and hatred raged. Neither winning, yet the anguish drew forth a fresh flood of slick. Peppering the air with the scent of a female in need. One conditioned to grow ripe at the slightest hint of cruelty.

"I must say," he continued, stripping off his leathers as honeyed lies spilled over his lips, "I'm impressed to find you alive. I was given every assurance there'd be no chance of your survival, but I knew." His mane rose up, aggression tightening against his nape, making the female cringe again. "How shall I punish you—"

She shook her head. "Hadim, *pl*—"

"Shhh," he whispered and caught a fist full of tangled, wet hair, and tipped her head back. Cradling her skull between deadly, extended claws. Gentle, to prepare her for the coming violence. "You went to great lengths to escape me, Omega, to escape your duty to my harem."

He smiled then, eager to lose himself in the limpid black gaze of a female in heat, to stoke her enticing temper into an inferno of hatred he could bathe in. Hers was a spirit that could cleanse his sins in the purifying heat of living flames—and all he had to do was wear Hadim's mask and let her believe her own lies.

An easy feat for one born to sit on the Karahmet throne.

"I'm suitably impressed. But now," he said, and let her feel the weight of his arousal, "I've come to collect what's *mine*."

It would be easy.

After all, Sinadim was his father's son...

Dazed, the war chief staggered and slipped on the wet rock, one foot left tangled in the netting. Head throbbing around a lump the exact shape of Sinadim's fist, his center of balance listed to the right. His senses sluggish, vision blurred.

But although his mind was foggy and his brain bruised, his body remembered its task. Hard and throbbing, straining toward the scent of slick and come, no matter that he was still ensnared.

With a scowl, Balkazar kicked his way toward freedom. Cursing and thrashing to rid himself of that thrice-damned netting.

An outraged snarl burst from his lips, for when he'd managed to blink the double vision away, it was to see none other than his treacherous Alpha hunched over a scrap of female flesh they were supposed to share.

Sinadim shunted into her from behind, a cruel gleam in his eye as she was made to brace on hands and knees. Hiccupping, tears ran freely down her face. The anguish etched in the tension between her brows, in the gritted, clenched teeth. Her ears pressed flat and nearly buried beneath the snarls of inky wet hair.

She was positively *glorious.*

And Sinadim was torturing her.

Refusing to set his knot. Grinning when she squealed and gushed around his girth, when she begged through the tears. Desperate for more.

"Give it up, Omega," Sinadim spat and snaked his arm beneath her chin. Caught her throat in the crook of his elbow and forced her back. To balance on her knees, hands scrambling for purchase while he sank deep into his haunches. Employing a leisurely pace, Sinadim sluiced through the frothy mess between her thighs with a toothy smile.

Breath coming hard, Balkazar's head cleared as Sinadim locked her against his chest. Adding leverage to choke, he made a fist in her hair. Growling when her dull, Hathorian claws dented skin, he squeezed until the veins on her forehead stood out in stark relief, her face beating red.

"I'm going to come again, little slut," Sinadim sang, lips pressed against her cheek, "and then you'll have to wait for relief... when all you have to do is"—he grunted, sweat tracing his temples—"submit."

He let her breathe, but she used the reprieve to hurl a savage, "Fuck you!" at the Anhur male capable of wringing her dainty neck without a bead of real effort.

Sinadim threw back his head and laughed. "Fine," he said and released a weak orgasm. Painting her insides white with ropes of sticky seed, while Balkazar was made to watch. To endure.

Shocked and concussed.

A tiny slip of a girl, denying an Alpha like Prince Sinadim.

Defiant, no matter the powerful scent of slick wafting through the air. The pain she must have been in to refuse whatever game Sinadim was playing instead of stuffing her full of his knot.

Something vicious bloomed in Balkazar's chest, and without an ounce of preparation or forethought, the war chief—a life-long student of discipline and strategy—charged. Blind with sick jealousy, with indignant fury, he aimed to attack a male he'd called *brother* for decades.

The squeals of a female in distress, the thick scent of rut that lingered on his palate, it incensed him. Fogged Balkazar's brain with rash aggression that needed only an outlet.

With a bellowing roar, he crashed into Sinadim's ribs.

The Alpha was torn from that soiled sheath with a *squelch* of fluids that splattered on the stone.

Gasping and shaking, the Omega collapsed. Curled into the fetal position, both hands darting between her legs as she writhed and whined. Keening, her brows drawn tight and pinched. Sweat streaking across blotchy red skin.

A delicious mess—and one Balkazar knew his Alpha had no intention of sharing. That he wouldn't honor their agreement without being forced.

Cock throbbing behind his leathers, the war chief cast a withering scowl at Sinadim. Attempted to take his share of their bounty and ease the ache pulsing in his sack. Meaning to inseminate the female they were supposed to share, the womb they were supposed to seed together.

He was struck down before he landed a single hand on her tempting body. Realizing too late exactly what state Sinadim was in.

The rut.

Blood thick with testosterone, the Alpha retaliated. A massive fist swung into Balkazar's peripherals, landed with a hollow ringing crunch that was white-hot where it slammed into his ocular bone.

Balkazar would not be denied, but to battle one such as Sinadim was a risk few could endure. Blind right eye or no.

With the advantage of a clear head, the war chief ducked the next swing and swept the Alpha's feet out from under him with a savage kick.

Sinadim fell with a dull thump, the wind rushing from his lungs with a pained grunt.

Before the other male could pull his dick from the dirt and think to fight back, Balkazar was on him.

He didn't mean to mark Sinadim. Hadn't intended to set his teeth in a mirror of the marks now speckling his shoulder—and he certainly hadn't intended to mount his Alpha. Hips flexing, cock twitching at the cage of leather breeches, they were kept separate even as they crossed a line never crossed before. But the urge to dominate overcame the war chief. Utterly.

With a final shake, he managed to tear himself away. Instead moving to pin Sinadim's forearm behind his back. "Remember our blood pact!" Balkazar bellowed, giving Sinadim one last chance to preserve their bond. Hackles raised in fury.

The Alpha huffed, shaking his head. Teeth dripping malice, fists clenched until they popped, only to snap open with claws fully extended. Leaving gouges in the red stone. Battling a powerful rut, the instinct to keep what he'd claimed. To kill.

"You can watch," Sinadim snarled, dangerous and regaining control. His eyes seething pools of black, trying to compromise without leverage.

"No." Cracking his neck, Balkazar hauled on Sinadim's forearm, making him arch. "You will honor the pact, *brother*. Equal shares.

Loyalty to the pack above all." He snorted, uttering a derisive scoff. "You'd trade all that for a breeder? *You?*" A smile broke through clenched and bloody teeth. Mocking. "You and she, against the wilds, huh? How will she fight your battles, I wonder? With what skills? What strength? We can always get more pussy," Balkazar said, "but without us, *my prince*, you will die with your knot stuffed in a sloppy cunt. *Alone.*"

For a moment, the Alpha continued to rumble with a low, threatening growl. And then, his mane flattening out, Sinadim coughed up a snarl. Tension riding high between his shoulders, but when he turned away, it was to expose his blindside. Good eye turned into the solid ground.

A subtle concession of willful trust.

Releasing his Alpha, Balkazar turned searing blue eyes upon the female he intended to punish.

Calmer and shaking it off, Sinadim turned back to the incoherent thing twitching in a puddle of sticky white fluid. Took a fist full of her hair and positioned her on all fours once more. And though he took liberties and slid his bloated prick back into her, he pried her jaws apart and offered the war chief the use of her throat.

Compromise Balkazar could live with.

As long as it was wet, female, and tight, it was good enough.

Freeing his aching girth, he wasted no

time. Dropping to one knee, he cradled the back of her skull in one large hand. Hauled her closer, made her stretch to taste the pearly drop oozing from his slit.

She groaned, lapping. Compliant, she hummed around his swollen knob, eyes dark and luminous. Glassy. Her every blink sluggish.

"I think this pretty little slut is come-drunk," Balkazar said, tilting her head back to peer into those deep, black pools. There was a layer of exhausted submission filmed over her lenses, but beneath it?

Banked flames of a defiant spirit.

A delicacy among the weak-willed Hathorians. An *Omega*.

One he would savor before breaking, but first?

"Were you trying to avoid being claimed?" Balkazar purred, pushing a hank of wet hair off her forehead as he stretched her lips. As Sinadim's pace increased, the tone of his growls becoming guttural as the Alpha neared orgasm. "Thought you would take from us and be allowed to walk away? That we wouldn't hunt until you were exactly where you are now. Where you belong."

Banked embers sparked to life, but Balkazar was ready. Before she bit his cock in half, he forced it down her throat. Keeping her jaws from closing with a tight grip on the hinge trying to snap shut and emasculate him.

"You'll be bred this night," he continued, presuming the fierce thing valued nothing more than her independence, for why else would she go to such lengths to avoid the An-hur? She, who taunted instead of submitting. "You need to learn your place, *Omega*," he cooed, insulting as he pulled back and seated his root between her canines. "You'll be well cared for. A cherished breeder kept fat with Beta soldiers."

Tears leaking from watery, black eyes, she coughed. Making Sinadim groan, his pace increasing. Unable to play games with the presence of another male so close, the Alpha pounded against her backside. Grip bruising the meat of slender hips, he roared. Seating himself one final time, shuddering as his knot began to bloat at last.

The girl went rigid, her throat vibrating around a gargled scream.

And it was enough.

With just enough forethought to wrap crushing fingers about his knot, Balkazar followed his Alpha into bliss.

25

Conversation rumbled around her.

The low vibrations of deep voices, though she couldn't make sense of the syllables. Not with a worthy knot rocking against her glands, the ache relenting at last.

A secret smile glazed her swollen lips, for she'd battled Hadim and won. An Alpha. Her master. She'd refused to beg, despite the torment. No matter that he'd demanded she bend to his whim, that there was another down her throat, or that she'd been claimed by her master once more—she endured the way she'd never been able in the harem.

And she'd *won*.

Something foreign swelled in her chest. A certain type of knowing that unfurled around her sense of self and wrapped it in blistering assurance.

Something she had no name for, though she wanted more.

"Pull your knot out. It's my turn."

The words fizzed inside her skull, sending tremors of worry clenching around the knot. Locking it in place. Her glands were not yet empty! The torment would come rushing back if he—

She felt fingers slipping around her opening. Squirming around his base, they prodded and broke the seal.

Fluid gushed between her thighs, wasted. *Wasted!*

Ears pressed flat, she bucked, freeing herself from the male before her. Turning to scowl at the one covering her back. "No! Don't—"

A fist wrapped around her throat. "No?" and it was the war chief who hissed at her, pressing close enough that she could taste his breath. "You're bold for an Omega, hmm?"

She tucked her chin, aiming blunted teeth at a thick wrist, but she was no match for Anhur reflexes.

With a snarl, the war chief hauled her up with one hand buried in her hair. Only by the grace of the Nine was she spared the agony of being torn off a knot—Hadim had enough purchase to compress his girth before they were forcibly uncoupled.

She squealed all the same. Deprived. Thrashing and kicking, she aimed for the naked flesh bouncing between the war chief's legs. Missed, and was spun around, her wrists caught between her breasts in one large fist.

"Let go!" she screeched, sticky heat twitching with renewed life against her lower back.

Against her cheek, a laugh. "As the lady wishes." And turning her out, the war chief let her stumble away.

Legs shaking hard enough to make her trip, she went down only a few steps away from the Anhur males. Landing in a heap of rubbery bones as they laughed, leering. Eyes darting between them—and their sex organs—she searched for help. For mercy.

There was only hunger looming above.

On the left, Hadim. Blinded in one eye. Mangled. He was the sadist who'd tortured her for years, but against whom she'd already won several small battles. The monster she knew well.

And on the right, his war chief. Second in command, his intentions toward her abundantly clear, but his methods an unknown. A horrible gamble she couldn't afford to take.

One male totally without his clothes, the other having only exposed himself for the express purpose of fucking her. Of breeding her and claiming his piece.

She scrambled back much too late. Just in time for a shadow to swallow her whole.

Terror made her turn, though she knew who caged her in.

The hybrids. Standing in a wall of bunching, gleaming muscle, their pupils black as coal, cocks swollen and needy once more.

She was trapped. Doomed to be the plaything of an entire pack run by Hadim.

Panic began to bubble in her guts, sending sweat to splash down her spine. It would be worse than her miserable life in the harem. At least then she'd had the support of misty blue eyes and a crinkly, weathered smile. In the harem, Hadim had only bothered her a few days every three months.

At least then she'd had yarrow root tea.

White-rimmed eyes flicked around the circle. Desperate for a champion to save her from this fate.

Stepping aside, Micah allowed Sickle to approach. Elegant tattoos the markings of a pampered pet who knew more about the highest fashion of Anhur culture than he did about the females of his own race. Sickle smiled, golden hair pushed back from his face, exposing more of the twisting designs staining his skin with blue ink.

"Please, miss," he murmured, showing the point of his teeth. The gesture not one of Hathorian pride, but a vehicle of hurt that only served to drive the difference between them home—her teeth had been filed short long ago. Robbing her of identity, of defense. Her mouth made to be nothing more than another wet hole that could be forced open and used.

A shiver ran over her skin, her muscles coiling. Preparing to flee.

"Miss," Sickle breathed, showing the flat of his palms. "Let us care for you. Please."

Ears laid back, she hissed.

"Let the Anhur ease your pain—"

She bolted, driven by pure instinct, she tried to run from these insidious lies. From the temptation of a caring embrace that would only hurt when it burrowed too deep and rotted where it lay, festering behind her ribs.

The war chief caught her about the middle, pulling at her as if she were an untried kit and not a seasoned whore who knew the burn of male flesh. Who didn't balk when it smeared across her belly. He pressed two fingers inside her, squelching in the mess. Making her glands lurch to clasp at the invasive digit.

But he withdrew before he could do more than tease, that sticky finger sucked clean as the war chief moved to embrace the rut, no matter Hadim's leavings. With a groan, he pressed closer and she caught a glimpse of blue eyes. Chips of frigid, hateful ice that made her gag. *Glassy. Pupils claiming slow millimeters of icy blue. One staring straight at her, the other twitching and lurching in the socket. Sightless...*

"*No,*" she hissed, shaking her head. Ears flicked back, her teeth bared.

Trembling, she tore her vision away from the specter of those beloved, *insidious* blue eyes. Looking instead to her hands—*hands*

*that were soaked to the elbow in blood, claws
curving around clumps of flesh and sinew... The
hands of a queen...*

She couldn't look away. Entranced by
shimmering phantoms too vibrant to be anything but a hallucination. A terrible nightmare she wished were more than a fever
dream. Unless...

Unless this double-sight was a prophecy
bestowed upon her by the Nine. A vision of
what she could become, if she would only
reach out and take it...

She blinked, blocking out the horror of
gore-spattered hands.

*Fingers pried apart were wrapped around a
cold, bony rope. Her tail. Inert, yet twitching.
Beautiful, black fur luxurious despite the blood.*

It felt so real.

And then she understood the meaning of
it all, what she had to do. What she'd been
born to do.

Assurance blistered her lungs on a held
breath. That something foreign returning to
harden her spine, blooming hot and fast,
making her chest swell with determined
courage. Surrounded by lies and no options,
her future was a blur of sticky, white endurance.

But only if she never asked for more.

"You will serve me," she whispered, lips
tracing the words, her voice all but absent as
she ran her fingers over the ghost of her tail.
Her eyes glassy and unseeing as she traced

the fine, elegant bones where they weren't. Where they'd never be again. But it didn't matter anymore because she *knew* what she was. *Who.* "You will serve me," she said, letting her memories fall with a splat of rejection, "because I demand it."

For a moment, there was only that.

The silent echo of their shock to hear a Hathorian speak of her needs. Her demands.

But she was far from finished. "Nest," she said, forcing the single word between clenched teeth. Her ears flattening as she braced for a fight. Hadim would have to deal with the messy Hathorian fluids he despised so much, but they would do this *her* way, in the custom of *her* people. "Take me to my nest."

This time she would use Hadim to satisfy her needs.

And then, when her season had ended, her glands deplete and satisfied... she would tear out his throat and trap his screams in her palm.

26

It was dark in her den.

Dank and wet. Atrocious ventilation, detritus littered the floor, every visible surface was coated with a fine layer of filth. It was little more than a cave—and one she'd probably commandeered from a forest beast. Knowing what little he knew of the wild, bossy little female, Sinadim had to presume she'd eaten whomever she'd found inside.

The thought of a Hathorian female so fierce and defiant made his cock throb, and he stroked it. Base to tip. Hungry for the moment when her eyes dulled, the fires banked in worship to *him*. When she went limp and pliant beneath the snapping hips of her new master, helpless to resist a natural season.

As if to remind him she had *two* masters, Balkazar pushed her forward, stripping free of his leathers with one hand. Beneath the war chief's foot, sticks and branches crackled. Crunched. Drawing a low, defensive hiss from female lips.

Frowning, his interest piqued, Sinadim watched her dart about. Wholly focused on setting her things right, on collecting the displaced treasures she'd amassed and returning them to their original position.

Not once did her inky gaze seek the exit. Never leaving the loose circle of random shit piled up in the darkest corner.

"Is *this* your nest?" Sinadim asked, lip curled. Understanding dawning as he saw the heap of forest litter with new eyes.

Saying nothing, the girl merely turned glassy black eyes up at him. Blinking acknowledgment, her cheeks pink. Fingers worrying a shard of speckled blue eggshell.

Edging closer, Sinadim abused that sacred space with all the arrogance his position of authority afforded him. His nostrils pinched white, he inhaled the musky scent of a female in season. Chest rumbling with satisfaction, his brain filled with pheromones. Crouched, he balanced on his haunches, left elbow braced over one knee. Reaching out with his free hand, he plucked the eggshell from dainty fingers. Inspected it with a concerned frown.

"Micah!" he barked. "Sickle! Gather our supplies. All the spare clothing and bedding you can find." And then he met her eyes. Happy to do battle with the little thing quivering with the exquisite, indignant fury of a female in heat. Who dared to order him about and whose nest had been violated. All her hard work, her obsessive organizing, dashed in a single swipe of one massive hand.

A squawk of protest ruptured her inky glare, leaving fatal cracks he would exploit to his advantage.

And with a sneer, Sinadim swept away the last of that sad excuse for a nest. Pleased to see her scramble after her precious treasures—utterly lost to her instinct—he confiscated sticks, leaves, moss, and other findings from the forest floor. His smile growing cruel. "It looks like our little bitch needs to learn to build a proper nest."

The female growled, the insult igniting her temper. Challenging her on a primal level, he continued. "Submission doesn't come easy to you, does it, Omega?" he asked and made her look. Forced her pretty face back with a fist in her midnight locks and caught her gaze in an unblinking glare.

"We'll teach her, brother," Balkazar said, prowling toward them. Cock in fist, he thumbed a pearly drop beaded at his tip. "She'll learn to serve on her back. Where she belongs."

At that, she transformed. In one instant, a softening female entranced by a male worthy of breeding her—in the next, a wild thing. Twisting and thrashing, she oozed from his grip. Launched herself at the war chief with a vengeance worthy of an Anhur queen. Her ripe state and nudity utterly forgotten.

And though Balkazar caught her easily, she continued to rage. Howling and untamed, leaving red streaks across the war chief's chest until he managed to catch her wrists. Until he spun her to face her Alpha and pressed against her back with a shudder of male satisfaction.

Sinadim grinned, for he would enjoy seeing her humbled before her season had ended. Filled and soiled. Marked with their scent. Their teeth and claws. The constant breeding triggering her eggs to drop so she might be seeded properly.

Pregnant.

Theirs forever.

Grinning, he touched his thumb to her bottom lip and nearly lost skin between the snap of blunt teeth. He was eager to see her broken in and tamed, tied to their every depraved whim. But a natural season posed certain... problems. Demanded the proper etiquette be followed, she would need to be enticed instead of *forced* to ovulate.

It was the ruling elite's greatest held secret, something Sinadim was sure even Balkazar didn't know. That during a natural season—one without suppressors forcing their hormones to spike, their eggs to ripen—Hathorian females could refuse to ovulate until a suitor pleased them.

Or simply not at all.

Micah and Sickle returned, the pack's worldly possessions slung over their shoulders. And with eyes downcast, they dumped their offerings outside of the nest. Clean and dirty underthings, unworn jackets, a spare roll of raw leather—it was all of it precious to a nesting Hathorian female.

Keeping his secrets, Sinadim simply watched when Balkazar released her, retreating to the outer edge of her nest. Content to observe as she rooted through their things. Selecting the finest leather with a dainty, high-pitched coo. A hum of approval she couldn't contain. Couldn't hide, for with a stuttering purr, she rubbed her face against the fine material.

Delight lit her features, altering her appearance once more. Displaying a glimpse of the obedient breeder she could be, Sinadim watched her twist in the worn leather. Turning in circles, her back flexing, then contracting where her tail would have been. Everything they owned coated in her scent, in the slick bubbling from her swollen slit.

It was a marvel. Ancient ritual no longer in fashion amongst the ruling Anhur, enthralling nonetheless.

"Take your fill before I seed her again, brother," Sinadim said, pumping his length from root to tip, the bulge of an eager knot twitching against his palm. "I won't wait much longer."

Weathered face splitting in a devious grin,

Balkazar lunged. A slender ankle seized in his fist despite the outraged squawk muffled inside that nest. The war chief caught her heel when it struck out at his face, both ankles captured and made to widen. Gooey petals peeled apart when her thighs were forced to spread, her face and chest left ensconced and buried.

"Beautiful," Balkazar groaned and pressed lips to her cunt. His tongue flicking back, over frilled labia and toward her clenching asshole, he scooped up every drop of slick he could reach. Nose mashing against her prominent clit, oblivious to the taste Sinadim had left gushing from deep inside. It was the only way to induce his rut. To taste her slick and keep drinking once he'd emptied himself. The ultimate male aphrodisiac so many of the ruling elite were addicted to.

Dainty hands settled on Balkazar's shoulders, bracing as he shifted and sucked that little bean into the heat of his mouth. Pushing against a male scumming to the rut, she was helpless against his need. Left to writhe as he nursed on swollen, engorged nerves, her legs flexed over his shoulders.

Sinadim paced around them, content to watch until the war chief withdrew. Robbing her of climax the instant her legs began to shake. Balkazar spread her then, showing Sinadim how her slit fluttered and clenched. Her *Biquea* glands inflamed, glowing red. Begging to be stuffed. Stretched and abused.

With a snarl, Sinadim shuddered. His mane bristling as he allowed another to take his place, fighting to honor the terms of the blood pact. To restrain himself. But it was a struggle, a war of endurance he was neither winning nor losing. On the surface, still, but for the stroking fist and twitching muscles. His mind, on the other hand, was a blur of rage. Fantasy and horror blending, he saw himself tear Balkazar's spine from his rib cage, drinking down yellow spinal fluid while the light in his eyes faded.

The breeder his, *alone*.

Shivering on the edge of madness, the Alpha approached with cock in fist, dropping to his knees at the edge of her nest. His chest vibrating with a prolonged, vicious growl. A warning he couldn't help issuing with Balkazar so near, the other male taking the female he'd already marked as his.

Eyes hooded as he worked her tight sheath, Balkazar took no notice. Accustomed to his Alpha's temper—especially with a breeding Omega.

Guessing where her head should be, Sinadim rooted around in the twisted leathers until his fingers encountered wet, ropey snarls of hair. He pulled and revealed the Hathorian's pretty face.

"You did a devious thing," Sinadim growled, scraping at her scalp with the tips of his claws. "Trying to evade us, to satisfy your heat without an Anhur knot?" He sneered, and tipping her face back, thrust forward. The tapered head of his prick smearing her lips with a sheen of want. "Your willful temper offends the Nine, *Omega*. And you'll be punished, but first"—he gazed into her heat-blackened eyes, letting her take a sip, pink tongue laving his slit—"you'll take my seed down your throat."

She whimpered as Balkazar filled her, not daring to so much as blink away from her Alpha. The male she thought was Hadim.

Bristling, Sinadim snarled down at her. Made her really look and see that his eyes were not the same shade as Hadim's. The slant of his brow, high cheek bones, and thick, sandy hair were all his mother's best features.

Defiance shimmered in her gaze. Sulky hatred, though she was properly enthralled. But not a hint of recognition beyond the dull hatred for her master.

Stooping, Sinadim lay a bruising kiss to swollen lips, then pried her jaws apart. Feeding her two fingers, he reached passed her gag-reflex. "You're going to let the war chief fill your pretty little pussy"—she gagged, flexing around Balkazar's shaft hard enough to make him gasp—"and then you'll take it in the ass." Sinadim paused, probing her throat while his second pumped between legs spread obscenely wide. Grinning as the battle to simply watch raged within. "We're going to keep you fat and lazy with Anhur sperm," he said, her throat making a squelching hiccup around invasive fingers. "Anywhere you've been touched before will be seeded *properly*. And what will you say after each knot?"

Little teeth flashed around his knuckles, her fury rekindled as she tried again to fight him—and Sinadim's cock jumped, connecting them with ropey strings.

"You'll say 'thank you,'" he said and made her lips part.

Wickedness gleamed in her black gaze, and she laved his tip, ears drooping in acceptance at last. "Thank you, Hadim."

Something in him snapped. To hear Hadim rewarded for *his* efforts? It frayed his temper at the edges, and it broke on a laugh. "I'm not your master, Omega," he snarled, feeding the length of his cock to the back of her throat until he felt his crown breach that tight ring. "And my father would never bother himself to come for you. One escaped harem slave isn't worth the effort," he spat, just to watch her eyes grow damp, hurt and confusion bleeding into watery defiance. "The Karahmet Heir has hundreds more just like you." Sinadim pulled her face toward his groin, borrowing deeper with a grunt. "One for every day of the year and two on holidays."

When she spluttered, he let her slide back. Her breath coming in heaving pants, eyes wide and rimmed in white as realization dawned in those glassy black pools.

"You belong to me now," he said, and dragged her lower lip down with his thumb, admiring the cut of blunted teeth. "And I want to hear you say my name."

27

She blinked. Confusion buzzing though her mind as the fog thickened and thinned in waves. Keeping pace with the rate of the war chief pumping her tight sheath, she existed in a blur of conflicting needs. At once a haze of lust and the shiver of painful revelation, for the monster wearing Hadim's face *wasn't* her master come to retrieve her.

It was his son.

She shook her head. *Impossible.* What he claimed was impossible because out of anyone, she would know—

"Sinadim," he murmured, tracing her lips with the tapered head of his cock. Thicker than she remembered. A different shade of red pulsed beneath the skin she'd thought she knew. "Say it."

Head shaking, ears tucked flat, she whined. Pulling back, she impaled herself on the war chief's prick, whispering, "Please...

please… please…" under her breath. Over and over, trying to wake up in her hidden den before this nightmare ever began. Before the confusion of heat had melted her faculties and she'd become what she feared most.

A cock sleeve, desperate to be filled.

Sobbing, she wished for the Nine to release her. To give her a cloak reeking of death she might use to slink away, because her only chance in reclaiming her freedom lay in her knowledge of *Hadim*. His habits and triggers.

But Hadim wasn't coming, and Sinadim was a dangerous enigma.

Unpredictable, for no matter that she'd managed to win a few meager battles, she was utterly unequipped to win a war.

And how could she? The Anhur were always ahead, always ready for the next rebellion before she'd even realized an injustice had occurred. Bigger, stronger, faster…

No, to fight was to be ruined by an unstoppable force. Hopeless and futile.

Trembling, she turned liquid eyes up and found not the face of a monster, but a male already lost to the rut. One who hadn't used excessive force, who stood before her fighting his composure just to hear his name spill over her lips.

There was power in his restraint. A dare to take her fill, to look at the male who meant to rule her and judge his worth for herself.

And though he glared—one blackened pupil blown wide, the other cast in silver and fixed in place—he made no move to force her obedience. Sinadim simply waited as Balkazar sluiced through that tight ring of glands, standing still as her gaze wandered.

Right cheek mutilated with the slash of four claws, the left a nightmarish reminder of the sire who'd tormented her dreams only half as badly as he'd terrorized her reality.

He was younger, perhaps not as wide in the shoulders as Hadim. Half a hand taller, and beneath the scars, she could see that his skin was darker now that she'd been given the chance to really look.

And his cock—it wasn't the one she'd carved from memory.

It was different. Long and thick. A drop of lust beaded at his tip, swelling before her eyes, until it ripened and burst. Spilling down the underside of a shaft riddled with juicy veins.

Sinadim was not his father.

He was a clean slate. A chance to be who she was inside, with a male who had no knowledge of who she'd been before. He hadn't hunted her with the intent to drag her back to the harem, to lop off her limbs and punish her with a gruesome gift of severed bone and sinew.

His needs were simple.

The rules in the beyond different because *she* demanded they change.

There was power in that, too. In knowing

his threats to deny her were meaningless, that their battle was one of endurance.

And who knew better than she how to mewl and present? How to please an Anhur male even without the aid of suppressors keeping her slick from spilling over. She'd been bred to endure in a way that the Anhur themselves had not.

In a grip that offered no room to squirm, Sinadim seized her jaw between forefinger and thumb. Mane standing on end, reeking of aggression, he pulled her closer, glaring with his good eye. "Say it, Omega!" he barked, voice edged in desperate need, the point of his claws prickling her skin.

Ingrained obedience saw her lips part— but it was laced with a something wicked. Something devious that decided not to fight, but refused to be a pet.

"Sinadim," she purred and lapped at his cock. Tasting him before an audience of males thick and engorged with want. "Mmm... You taste good, Sinadim."

Fingers tightened in her hair, and Sinadim pressed forward with a groan, forcing her to take his girth down her throat. "Good girl," he whispered, his jaw going slack. Eyes glazed and hooded.

Why should she fight when it was so much easier to coo and squirm? When the show of submission would grant her leniency without wasting a moment of effort.

"And what's your name?" she hummed,

twisting to make eye contact with the male rutting at her back when Sinadim next allowed her to breathe. Emboldened by the taste of Anhur semen on her tongue, by the hint of authority crackling through her veins.

Chest rumbling, the war chief forced a breathy, "Balkazar," through his teeth, hiking her thigh over his hip as he made space between her knees.

The muscles of her back flexed where she would have flicked her tail. Invitation for a worthy suitor.

But she had no tail to lift, and so it couldn't be used as leverage while she was held trapped beneath Anhur claws. And in that, she found another sort of freedom.

"Fuck me," she breathed, the simple act of making demands enough to make her head spin. "Breed me, Balkazar. If you think you can…"

"What—" Balkazar barked, fucking her all the harder.

"Leave it," Sinadim snapped, and must not have been impressed by her guile. With claws extended, he reclaimed her attention with a throaty snarl, aiming to silence her with cock until she offered up a dainty purr. Feminine, light and breezy, she purred a song of submission and deceit for Hadim's son. Swallowing his prick until his scowl eased and his fingers went slack in her hair. The aggression bleeding from tense muscles as she drank him in and swallowed him down.

With a gasp, she felt Balkazar thicken. The state of her *Biquea* glands too much for anything but an Alpha, a war chief was outmatched by a lowly Omega. Balkazar's breath hitched, flexing until he pressed against that final gate. Speared against her cervix, the point of his cock trying to force her open, to accept what he had to offer and seed that precious, rare womb.

Unworthy.

She rejected him with a crush of her glands, and Balkazar snarled, picking up an erratic, wild rhythm that saw his hips clap against her ass. Forcing broken little squeals of mounting pleasure to tear free of her throat and vibrate around Sinadim's prick.

Back arching, Balkazar seated himself one final time. Going deep enough to bend his rod where he could go no further, he came, pumping her full of with a shudder. Claws extended where they sank into the meat of her hips. Her thighs.

It wasn't enough.

"More," she whispered, withdrawing to kiss the Alpha's tip. Her breath warm, ears laying soft and submissive. "Sinadim, *please.*"

"As you wish," Sinadim said—purring deep and cocky—and tore Balkazar out of her cunt before his knot could fully balloon inside her.

Wasting the last of his seed, Balkazar stained the sparse hairs on her mound with ropes of pearly white and fell back. Laying sprawled in her nest, his long fingers tracing the length of a rigid prick coated in a creamy glaze.

She wasn't given a moment to catch her breath before Sinadim was on her. Dragging her slender naked form against his chest, the Alpha wrapped a hand about her throat. Cradling her vitals, his touch was gentle, claws merely denting her skin when she didn't bother to fight his touch.

At her back, she felt Sinadim shudder, felt the primal urge to claim her depths for his own as it rattled through his big frame. Through the heavy slabs of muscle where they quivered above and around her.

"You think to claim me?" she whispered, lips softening around the edges, words rattling against his palm. Ears leveling out as she relaxed against his heat. Melting against his thigh. "You think to breed me when your father couldn't?"

Sinadim went stiff. His breath caught where his heart thudded against her spine.

And then a single bark of laughter snapped against her nape, and the Alpha squeezed her until her ribs creaked in protest. Her breath *whuffed* over her lips as she was lifted from her nest, squirming. Desperate to burrow.

"What a treasure you are," Sinadim hummed, keeping her spread and exposed for the pack to see. A sharp smile was pressed beneath her jaw before he licked the tendon connecting shoulder to neck.

A subtle threat. An insult to her heritage, for only Hathorian males, with their pointed canines, were known to leave mating bites—and only then, when it was a committed pairing. A bond meant to last until death.

"Should I?" Sinadim whispered and switched her collar to his off hand while the other wandered. His calloused palm rasping over reddened, bruised nipples. Over the taut skin of her belly and beyond. "Would you gush for me if I mark you, Omega?"

An unexpected squeal burst from her lips, for when he cupped her mound, it was to grind the heel of his palm against her clit. Long fingers parted folds drenched with slick and come, tracing her where she ached.

"Don't worry, pet," he murmured. "I'll give you what you need."

She laughed then, goading the male who grinned against her cheek. "Do your worst, *Alpha*. I have no fear of the Karahmet males."

Thick fingers plunged into her depths, squelching and squishing as they wriggled. He whipped her aching glands into a lather as she sagged against his forearm. Pinned to his chest, moaning.

Helpless.

With a gasp, she tried to lurch away before her glands clenched around the invasive digits and shattered her control.

"Brave little Omega," Sinadim hummed

and pulled away from her pussy. Tracing her lips with fingers that glistened with seed and drove her straight into depravity. "Trying to sound bold, when all you really want is a knot."

She hummed, throaty and full of challenge. "Any knot would do."

A growl rumbled against her ear, and Sinadim set his teeth to her shoulder. Pinching. Not hard enough to break skin... but enough to send a torrent of fresh slick to wet her thighs. Enough to make her whine and shake.

"*Please*." She tucked her chin, trying to protect the space meant for a Hathorian mate, even as she gushed in perverse pleasure. "Don't."

Nudging her ankles apart, Sinadim relented with a kiss against her pulse. A smirk flickered against her throat, his breath heated as it dampened her skin. And then, hips rocking against her backside until his knob found her sodden folds, Sinadim fucked the gap between her thighs. Spearing through the frothy mess and bumping his knuckles on the other side, Sinadim walked her forward. Making her ride his shaft with each step she took, he drove her toward Balkazar. Still laying in the twisted leathers coated in the scent of sex, the war chief stroked his cock, eyes blazing with heated interest as they approached.

"You're going to lick him clean, little slut,"

Sinadim growled, fucking her thighs at a leisurely pace. "And you're going to take every inch of this dick until you are stained inside and out with my scent."

A mad grin spread across her lips. Her ears low, but not back. Tucked and ready.

"Nasty temper for a breeder," Balkazar said, lip curled, cruelty in every downward stroke of his fist. In the angry flash of purple-red where his knob peaked between his fingers.

Sinadim didn't give her a chance to rebel, he caught a fist full of wild black hair and made her twist to meet his disfigured grin. "There will be time enough to exorcise our wildling's rebellious nature," Simadim said, and shoved her toward Balkazar's shining prick. "And when she's fat with a litter of hybrids, I will teach her what it means to be Omega."

Defiance glittered in her black gaze, but with a soft sigh, she took Balkazar's cock between her lips. Drinking deep of what spurted from his tip.

"Take it then, little slut," Balkazar growled and sat forward. Feeding his girth into her throat even as he reached for the globes of her ass and spread her cheeks with big hands. "You were born to be nothing but a hole." He hooked his forefingers inside her opening, making her gape for Sinadim. Lewd and on display for the Alpha. "Nothing but a nice, tight quim to be filled with seed," the war chief rumbled, rocking his hips as his tapered head pressed against the back of her throat. "You were meant to breed hybrids for the Silver City, and now"—the blunt head of Sinadim's prick pressed against her pussy—"you'll breed for *us*."

She hummed, a smile quirked around Balkazar's girth. It was nothing to let him think so, because some part of her heat-addled brain had been conditioned to want that too. She *wanted* them to lose control and fight each other for the exclusive right to breed her. To snarl when she begged and see only to their own satisfaction...

"Does that surprise you, Omega?" Sinadim asked. "That I would share you with another?"

She wasn't given opportunity to answer—Balkazar's hand clapped against the back of her head, keeping her impaled as Sinadim pumped his shaft at her seam. Teasing. Pushing the limit of her restraint as he denied them both.

But she didn't beg or squirm. Oh, no. Not when she knew Sinadim couldn't last long like that, not with the amount of slick gushing from her depths. It was an enticing lure no Anhur male could possibly resist—least of all one of the Karahmet bloodline.

Instead, she snaked one hand between Balkazar's legs and cupped his heavy sack. Redoubling her efforts, she ignored the

Alpha and worked instead to shame the war chief with an early spilling.

Balkazar, who thought she was nothing. Who was about to learn a lesson. She issued a warning with the scrape of blunt teeth dragging along his shaft.

"None of that," Sinadim whispered and mounted her at last. Forcing his cock through her glands, she was made to take it, inch by agonizing inch. He didn't stop until he was seated within her, the early flare of his knot beginning to swell where it was stuffed inside her.

Groaning, she felt her sheath melt around him, molding to fit as he bullied his way through aching tissue.

He slapped her ass hard enough to make her flinch, the impact ripples felt all the way to the base of her spine. Where her docking scar tingled and flexed.

With a hiss of held breath, Sinadim bucked into her depths. His engorged tip pressed at her cervix, demanding entry. "I'm going to come so deep inside you that I won't have to bother with a knot," he whispered, covering her back. Lips brushing against the fuzzy shell of her ear. "It'll take a week for you to stop dripping, but by then." He paused to lave her shoulder with the flat of his tongue, gently sluicing through wet folds as she shuddered beneath him. "By then, your belly will already be full of my kits."

Muscles seized in anticipation, she went

stiff, ensnared by his threats. Glands bearing down to reject his knot or milk it dry…

"It won't be long before you begin to swell with a litter of hybrids," he said, fucking her hard and deep. Long, full strokes that clapped against her ass. "*My* litter."

She merely smiled as she was used from both ends, for though her skin was speckled with fingerprints, her insides deliciously bruised, she felt him swell and knew her victory was at hand.

With the pack all around them, it was like the days of long ago. The days before her species was enslaved by the Anhur, when a natural season was a cherished celebration of fertility, and their males were enough. Harkening back to those long forgotten Hathorian ritual matings witnessed by an entire pack, she'd claimed her males in a nest of her making.

Sweating freely, Sinadim fucked her with wild abandon, his breath hot, grip unyielding. Rutting her like the savage he was.

Anhur right down to the very root, she felt Sinadim beginning to stretch and expand within her. Unfurling not with the jerky fervor of the lesser males, but with a lazy, confident pulse.

"Please, Alpha!" she cried, tearing free of Balkazar's cock to twist, straining to meet Sinadim's good eye. "I want your knot," she demanded, ears standing forward. Eyes blazing, her cheeks pinkened with the rush of command. That the Alpha met her eye and roared, drilling into her with a fury she'd never felt before.

That he *obeyed*.

Snarling, Sinadim went still inside her, his orgasm building as his knot grew, bulging thicker with every frantic thrash of his heart. Expanding until—with a great rush of liquid fire—her glands burst, expressing the soothing agent that would ease her torment at long last.

Wailing, she came apart between them. Split. Soaking Sinadim's crotch with slick, she howled and fucked him back. Panting when Balkazar's fist tangled in her hair as he held her still, his fist rolling over his knob as his balls drew tighter and tighter. His knuckles bruising her lip as they skimmed her teeth.

"Open," Balkazar snarled and set the tip of his cock to her lips. Jerking his shaft in a desperate blur.

Mindless, convulsing with pleasure, she took him in, purring as she came. Her every spare drop of attention fixed to the knot milking her glands dry. She hardly noticed when the war chief grunted and filled her mouth with gush after gush of salty sperm— she swallowed. An ingrained reflex to nurse at the underside of a cock as it jerked and kicked.

But Sinadim hadn't finished.

Thrusting as far as he could, Sinadim barked, "Take it, Omega!" and dropped his weight across her back. His orgasm splattering across the roof of her cunt, he locked inside her for the second time.

She sobbed as her glands were drained. The orgasm that shuddered through her was a thing not felt before. Surging in time with every pulse spraying her full, she was bred docile. Drunk on Anhur seed, her face wet with tears.

For a moment, there was nothing but heavy breathing. Broken gasps, racing hearts, and the eyes of the pack gleaming in the darkness of her den.

A smile flickered in the gloom, lips swollen, but teasing and playful where they crinkled at the edges. Almost coy as she glanced at the Alpha from beneath the fan of thick dark lashes. And settling her cheek on Balkazar's thigh, she arched her back, pressing into Sinadim's knot. "More," she commanded, her voice husky with the ring of authority. Absent any hint of desperation, for she didn't have to beg. She would take from males desperate to give.

As a queen should.

And why not?

This was a test of endurance.

The rules hers to change at a whim. Theirs to obey.

"Again," she said and sucked Balkazar's tip back into her mouth.

28

He'd run through the night. Following the river, his every sense primed for a whisper of slick on the breeze. The hunter hadn't dared to slow, for none knew better than he the sort of monsters who roamed these wilds.

It wasn't until the sun kissed the horizon that he heard it. The desperate sounds of a female in distress.

No longer following his nose, the hunter raced toward those desperate screams. Sprinting toward an uncertain outcome, he was driven by the unmistakable knowing that his mate was being bred by another. A small pack, by the sounds of male voices ringing out in answer to her sweet, warbling calls.

Teeth flashed in the dark, and the hunter redoubled his effort. White lather dripping down his nape as he flew between tree trunks. Darting and weaving, he abandoned all efforts at stealth. Clinging to every sound she made, her every muffled squeak and guttural moan a symphony of hope.

After all, the dead rarely bothered to make such beautiful sounds.

And so it was that the hunter burst through the trees and found himself heaving for breath at the edge of a rocky clearing. Situated at the base of a cliff, the wind was stained with the scent of rutting, *healthy* males. Those not infected with Trax, their bodies mutated beyond all recognition.

So thick in the air it almost masked the hint of slick twisting on the breeze.

A shriek came from a dark cavern nestled at the foot of a sheer rock face. Long and low, she wailed, an orgasm stretching her vocal cords to their limit. Ending on a sob for more that went unanswered.

The hunter cracked his neck, amber eyes gleaming. Muscles trembling with scarcely contained fury, his cock aching for release. Ready for a battle, yet leery of challenging so many males at once—that his female might be torn apart in the fight.

No, this was a task that required stealth. Cunning and careful, precise timing.

He loped around the clearing, slinking through the shadows at the forest's edge until he spotted two hybrid males. One black, the other tan, both naked. Already used, they lay slumped and panting at the mouth of the cave. Barely conscious.

Lips peeled back from his teeth, the

hunter's matted mane began to bristle. Musk all but dripping from his skin as his temper rose in waves of rigid tension. Luminous amber eyes fixed to the throbbing pulse fluttering at the base of hybrid throats. The swarthy, dark skin stretched over the artery, glistening in the sun...

Flexing his fist just to feel his claws press into the meat, he inhaled all the way to the bottom of his lungs. Held the breath until it began to ache, then released it. Inching closer with precise, economical movements, his claws extending.

Movement from the cave caught his eye, and he retreated. Choosing to wait and watch.

Slender, pale flesh reddened by a long night of rut. Her eyes pools of liquid darkness, she darted free of her den. Stepped over the sprawled legs of two hybrid males. Skulking on the balls of dainty feet, she slipped from their grasp without a sound, a wicked smile etched in place as she stopped at the mouth of her den. Looking back.

When her fingers darted down, into the dark triangle of thatched hair, the hunter's cock beat at his restraint. Warring with fascination to see so slight a creature daring to linger when she should have been running.

Unable to tear his attention away from what would soon be his, the hunter watched with wide eyes as she painted the rock with grand, sweeping letters.

And there, in the sheen of early morning

light, a word shimmered above the exhausted pack. Painted in a pearly glitter of dried fluids, it shone in the lingering glow of the planet's three moons. A signature that read simply: *Renegade.*

Throat rumbling, the hunter let her go. Standing guard as she dressed herself from a stash of hidden supplies, produced a short spear, and escaped the pack who'd tried to keep her. Blending seamlessly with the shadows of the wood.

After all... there was nothing quite like the thrill of chasing prey that had a head start... and this prize was one worth killing for...

****Psst. Hey you! Click here for a secret, NSFW version of the incredibly hot cover of this book... trust me, you don't want to miss this... It's filthy enough that you'll be wondering... "Can I get pregnant from this??"****

Thank you for reading *Renegade, The Feral Court Book 1.*
Turn the page for a full chapter sneak peek of *Giaus, The Feral Court, Book II!*

Grab your copy of Giaus today!

GIAUS

Grab your copy of Giaus today!

Feet flashing over the detritus, a lone female fled through the forest.

Sprinting with the winds of retribution snapping at her heels. Yet affixed to her lips?

A smile that was both breathless and feral, for she had just proven she was not like others of her kind.

The Hathorian breeders, slaves to Anhur masters simply because of their ability to spawn a litter of strong, infertile soldiers who were born to bend the neck.

But she was an enigma. Other. A renegade.

The Renegade.

She'd refused to succumb to her first natural season, battled a prince and his entire pack to take what she needed—and she'd *won*.

No longer was she the vulnerable harem

girl begging the Nine to grant her freedom. A nameless Omega whose worth amounted to nothing more than a warm hole dripping with potent slick.

She had a name—one she'd chosen herself.

One that fit.

Renegade grinned, her ears tipped forward and stiff. Her lower back bunching where her tail would have been held high in salute, a bristling flag flown in tribute to an arrogance she'd been made to earn.

No, she wasn't like the other Omegas. Her harem sisters, each a semi-precious commodity with an expiration date branded on the inside of her womb. Where they were soft and delicate, Renegade was wire-wrapped velvet.

Always had been.

The matron had told her so.

And she'd taken an entire pack to prove it. Made her demands of Hadim's outcast son, then simply... left. And it had been easy— Sinadim and his war chief had been so fuck-drunk, they'd allowed her to slip free from the tangle of limbs. Allowed her to flee into the night, her heat satisfied, Biquea glands no longer engorged.

And why shouldn't she? To stay was to become the first precious gem in Sinadim's new harem. Mounted daily, she'd be filled to over-flowing, then filled again. And again. And again until she was drunk on sperm and couldn't remember that she loved to create. Until she forgot the joy of molding clay with her hands and giving life to the fantastic creatures who lurked in her dreams.

A sneer twisted her lips.

What need had she of Anhur males who couldn't force her to stay? She, who hunted when her belly growled and found a new den every night without fail. Always roaming. Lawless. And when her cunt ached? Satisfaction would be her choice, *her due*, because she demanded it.

She would not suffer being kept as their pet, beholden to rejects like Sinadim and Balkazar. Caged in the same den, night after night, forced to raise their kits and mewl when they wanted to fuck.

Ears flat, she bolted into the underbrush, sprinting flat-out. Leathers whispering over her thighs as she slipped through the shadows. Feet sure, muscles limber, she ran until her forehead grew damp with a fine, dewy sheen, but she would not slow. Couldn't. After all... she'd gotten what she'd set out to get.

This was the price.

Renegade had a head start—one she'd bought with her pussy and mouth and every last centimeter of cunning she possessed. One she couldn't waste. It wasn't much, considering the size and skill of the males who'd be coming for her, the achy twinge that begged her to return to that soiled nest of leathers and males. But it was enough.

It had to be enough.

As if to mock her defiance, something behind her crashed through the brush. Moving at speed. Trailing her and making no effort toward discretion.

A strangled cry ripped free from her throat. Heart skipping over her ribs hard enough to make her stumble.

How? How had they managed to catch up to her so quickly? And without making a sound?

A roar blasted through the thinning forest. Startling an earnest scream from her lips, for in that single, fleeting instant, she knew exactly what hunted her. That it wasn't Sinadim's ragged pack, but something else. Something much worse, and she knew then just how foolish she'd been in abandoning her defensible den filled with possessive pack males, fuck-drunk and ready to die for nothing more than another taste of her slick.

Heart in throat, she didn't turn. Didn't grace the hunter with even the slightest glance, or broadcast her spine-bending terror —she merely redoubled her effort to flee.

It wasn't nearly enough.

Bellowing, the hunter crashed through the thinning trees at her back, closing the distance between them in massive, ground-eating strides. Driving her to the edge of the wood, he pushed her beyond anything that might be used for shelter. Any fleeting shred of sanctuary she might have sought, and in doing so, eliminated any obstacles she might have put in his path.

He had, in fact, left her nothing in the way of options—beyond the forest, there were only gently rolling hills. Nothing to be used in defense but the startling certainty that she'd been herded.

But the realization came too late, and Renegade didn't have the time or breath to scream before the hunter took a swipe. Kicking her boots out from under her, the hunter sent her tumbling to the forest floor in a confused heap of limbs. It was only by the grace of the Nine that she rolled to the left instead of right, for with a snarl, the hunter charged right on past her. Unable to stop or change direction as quickly as someone who'd had the incredibly good luck to be stopped by the trunk of a young tree.

On her feet before the pain could register, Renegade did the only thing she could—she went up.

Pulling herself over the lowest branch, she flung herself into a sturdy sapling and reached for the next branch above it.

The hunter roared again. Rattling her bones and eardrums as she crested the second rung in her makeshift ladder and narrowly avoided another swipe—this one aimed at pulling her bodily from the tree and back to the earth. Where she'd be utterly at the whims of fate. At his mercy.

Renegade couldn't help the terrified little

squeal that burst from her lips. Couldn't help the tremor in her hands as she climbed or stop her thoughts from once again returning to the pack. But it wasn't until the hunter jumped—missing the first branch entirely as he clung to the second—that Renegade screamed for help. That she called for her rejected pack and wished for the dull safety a functional unit could offer.

The male bending the back of her fragile sapling was anything but safe, and when Renegade had climbed as high as she could, there was nothing left but to look.

To acquaint herself with the male who would surely be her doom.

His fur was a mess of mats and burrs, though beneath it all she could tell it might have once been beautiful. He was unkempt—as true ferals usually were—and big. Really, *really* big. Easily the weight of two Anhur males combined, this feral was Alpha straight down to his core. She could smell it on him as he struggled to reach her and scale her tree in one smooth movement. Couldn't ignore the scent of his pheromones that hung heavy on the air, or unsee that impressive bulge distorting the front of tattered pants.

It was his eyes that truly caught her attention. Gold. Streaked with green and flecks of chocolate. The mark of a feral. Of the infected.

But this was no simple Anhur male.

The Trax virus had marked him. *Deeply.*

He was a mutant, his genes warped, his nature altered only half as much as his body, for the beast was easily as big as one of her hybrids—and twice as stupid.

There would be no reasoning with this beast. There would be no compromise, discussion of mutual satisfaction, or foreplay, for the Trax had taken his mind. If he caught her, he'd take exactly what he wanted. He'd try to plant a litter in her womb, and rut her until Renegade was little more than a sleeve for his drooling cock.

Addicted to feral sperm.

Keening, Renegade whined, her gaze turning back, to the pack she'd abandoned.

And she prayed.

Grab your copy of Giaus today!

ALSO BY MYRA DANVERS

Swallowed by Darkness ~ **FREE**

- Grab your free copy of Swallowed by Darkness now!

The Last Tritan

- Flame to Frost, The Last Tritan, Book I
- Frost to Dust, The Last Tritan, Book II
- Dust to Smoke, The Last Tritan, Book III

Tritan Evolution

- Ravenous Innocence, Tritan Evolution, Book I
- Insatiable Corruption, Tritan Evolution, Book II
- Lavish Destruction, Tritan Evolution, Book III

The Feral Court

- Renegade, the Feral Court, Book I
- Giaus, The Feral Court, Book II
- Sickle, The Feral Court, Book III

Atom and Evil

- Delirium, Atom and Evil, Book I

MYRA DANVERS

USA Today Bestselling author, Myra Danvers, is best known for her compelling mix of unique science fiction and dark fantasy worlds that feature feisty heroines, antihero men, and of course, proper villains. Though you may not always know who is who until the final pages...

- facebook.com/MyraDanvers
- instagram.com/myradanvers
- bookbub.com/profile/myra-danvers
- goodreads.com/httpwwwgoodreadscom-myradanvers

9 781989 472163